The Salt Pirates of Skegness

Chris d'Lacey

Illustrations by Korky Paul

ORCHARD BOOKS

Chapter One

"Great-Aunt Hester's?" Jason groaned, as if his mother had just told him he was going to the dentist to have all his teeth removed. "But Mum, we only went last Saturday!"

Mrs Webberly offered him a simpering grin. "Think of it as an unexpected treat."

Jason screwed up his nose. It would be a far bigger treat if he never had to go to his aunt's house again. Aunt Hester was a grouchy old stick of a woman. She had purple-rinsed hair, blue-lensed glasses and whiskers growing out of a mole on her chin. She lived in a house called Shingle Towers beside the wind-blown sea front at Skegness. That was the only decent thing about her.

"Blame Kimberley," Mrs Webberly added, throwing some clothes into the washing machine. "Your dear little sister somehow managed to come away with one of Aunt Hester's perfumes last weekend, and I said we'd return it."

Jason looked doubtful. Perfume? Aunt Hester? She always smelled of stale fish and cat wee to him. "Can't you post it?" he said.

"No," said his mum. "Aunt Hester says the perfume is very precious. She doesn't want the bottle broken open in the post. Oh yes, that reminds me..." She pointed at the shopping bags leaning up against the door of the fridge. They were bulging with all sorts of empty jars and bottles.

Jason sighed. It was one of his weekly chores to take cans and bottles to the local recycling point. Like any chore, he hated it. "Why do *I* always have to go?" he moaned.

"Because, my little *poppet*, you're such an expert at smashing things."

Jason scowled darkly. He knew his mum was talking about the pane of glass in Mrs Willoughby-Wallace's cucumber frame. Mrs Willoughby-Wallace lived next door. She didn't approve of 'pesky little boys'. Especially those who liked to try out their dads' new golf clubs in the long school holidays.

"Don't be long," his mother said trimly. "You know what else happens on Fridays, don't you?"

At that, Jason's spirits took a real nosedive. "You're horrible to me," he grumbled. He hoisted up the bags and clanked the bottles down the garden path. Friday night was BIG bath night. Toenails clipped. Hair wash. The lot. If it wasn't for the fact that it was always fish fingers for tea on a Friday, Jason thought he might have run away from home years ago.

The recycling point was at the local park. There were three big bottle banks there. They looked like fat plastic tubs with big round portholes where the bottles went in. There was a white tub for clear bottles, a green one for green bottles, and a brown one for brown bottles.

With a sigh Jason put down the bags and started to take the bottles out. They were nearly all clear ones. He reached up and pushed the first bottle down the middle hole of the white tub. It made a lovely crashing sound. This was the only bit of the chore that Jason liked: smashing the bottles, hard. He liked aiming them through the centre of the holes. Sometimes he played a sort of game with himself, scoring points if a bottle didn't hit the sides of a hole too many times on its way into the tub. If a bottle went through cleanly, that was worth a full ten points.

He was still trying to achieve his first ten point chuck

when his hand closed around a small, pear-shaped bottle unlike any he had seen before. It was a strange turquoise colour for a start, which called for a tricky decision about the best tub to aim it down (he eventually chose the green). The glass was peculiar too. It had a sort of *scaly* feel, as if the contents of the bottle had at one time spilled and left a crusted residue behind. It reminded Jason of the time he and his dad had visited the War Museum and Jason had picked up a hand grenade. "What you had to do was pull out the pin and throw it really quick," his dad had said, "then *poom!* it exploded." A hand grenade. That's what Jason imagined the bottle could be. He would pull out the fancy stopper, throw the bottle in and hear it explode – *poom!*

The only problem was, no matter how he tried, he couldn't pull out the stopper. He steadied the bottle between his knees and had a go; he wedged the stopper under a flagstone and levered; he even tried tugging it free with his teeth. No way was that stopper going to leave that bottle. Jason shrugged. It didn't matter. The bottle grenade would still make a really good bang when it went. He stepped up to the green tub and let it fly.

Poom! The splintering crash of glass invaded the peace of the summer's day. But there was another noise too: the noise of a squeaky, distant voice.

"A-haar!" it cried. "Stand by to be boarded!"

There was a whoosh of wind inside the bottle bank and a peculiar smell of seaside air.

Jason Webberly stood absolutely still, gawping at the hole where the bottle had gone. Had he heard a voice? Or had he just imagined it? He took a quick glance around. On the verges of the park, a few pigeons were pecking gently on the grass. But there was no one else at the recycling point. Jason pressed his ear to the bottle bank and listened. From somewhere deep within came the swish of waves and…was that the screech of a gull he could hear? It had to be a trick, surely? He shrugged, grabbed a wine bottle and fired it through the nearest hole.

There was a dull sort of clonk inside the bottle bank and an angry voice cried: "Jumping plates of jellyfish! Attacked!" And just as quickly as it had gone into the hole, the bottle came flying out again. It hit the paper bank on the other side of the compound and shattered into several sharp-sided pieces.

Jason Webberly stood back a pace. This time he didn't need to be convinced. There was definitely *something* inside the bottle bank. And he'd just chucked a wine bottle at it.

He started to quiver. He started to quake. He could

hear his front teeth chattering, "Mu-um..." But it was all too late. Before he could think of running away, a wispy stream of whitish dust came whistling out of the bottle bank. It twisted through the air like the tail of a tornado and began to form into a human figure.

"Help," whimpered Jason and covered his eyes.

"A-haar!" a throaty voice cried. "Free as a freckle at last!"

Jason peeked through the cracks of his fingers.

There was a pirate standing in front of him.

Chapter Two

He was old and bowed and *incredibly* filthy. He had yellowing teeth, clogs on his feet, a patch across one eye, and a red and white scarf knotted round his forehead.

No doubt about it, definitely a pirate.

"Who be you?" the pirate demanded, pointing a grubby finger.

"I be— I mean— I'm J-Jason," Jason spluttered. "W-where did you come from? Do you live in there?"

The pirate turned and looked at the tub. "I be out of my bottle," he beamed.

"Bottle?" squeaked Jason. "You came out of that *bottle*? You mean, you're a genie?"

The pirate knitted his one good eyebrow. He didn't seem to understand the meaning of 'genie'. "I be a

11

fearsome seadog!" he raked. "Stand by to be boarded! The stone be mine!"

Jason bit his lip, not sure what to do. Although he'd never been to sea, he was pretty sure you needed a ship to be 'boarded'. And what 'stone' was the pirate on about? The only stones that Jason could see were tiny pieces of gravel on the tarmac. "I'm sorry," he gulped. "I don't know what you mean."

The pirate, too, looked a little confused. He scratched the bump on his head where the wine bottle had hit him. "I be boggled," he muttered. "Blown off course." He cupped a hand above his eyes and peered around. "Which way be the sea, boy? For'ard or aft?"

This wasn't an easy question to answer. Jason lived in Leicester, the middle of the Midlands. The sea was miles away – on all sides. Just his luck to encounter a fearsome seadog here. "I think the nearest place is Skegness," he said.

The pirate's eyes nearly popped from their sockets. "That's where I be headed, boy! Be you knowing a fair passage? How be the tides in these landlubbing parts?"

Jason shuffled his feet. "We don't have tides here, only canals. You can't *sail* to the seaside. You have to go in the car."

Now it was the pirate's turn to look confused. "What

vessel be that? How many men do it take to row it?"

"You don't *row* it," said Jason. "It's a sort of…chariot. A bit like a boat on wheels." At that moment, a single-decker bus came rumbling past, brushing the branches of the trees by the gates.

"Suffering seashells!" the pirate cried, and hid himself behind a rubbish bin.

"That was a chariot," Jason explained, wondering how old the pirate was. He clearly didn't know about modern transport – but he didn't seem all that fazed by it either. Now the initial shock had passed, he looked like a child on its first real Christmas.

"You have such a chariot?" he gibbered excitedly, stroking his whiskery chin.

"My dad does. We're going to Skegness in our…chariot tomorrow."

The pirate's eyes lit up like lamps. He immediately started to dance on the path and sing a happy, wheezy song:

I'm on me way, me hearties!

I'm out of me bottle I am!

I be as swell as the sea in a seashell!

As clever as a crab in a clam!

I am, I am, I am, I am, I am, I am, I am...

"A-HEM," Jason interrupted loudly, after about the tenth *I am.* "*You* can't come. I can't take a mucky old pirate home. Mum'll go mad."

The pirate jumped down to Jason's side. "But shipmate, I must sail seaward soon, else I be cursed for ever and a day."

A pit began to form in Jason's stomach. Cursed? That smacked of witches and nasty spells and things any sensible boy would rather not know about. But what could be worse than being imprisoned in a turquoise bottle? And who'd put the pirate in there, anyway? Jason swallowed his fears and asked.

"'Twas the Skegglewitch!" the pirate blasted in reply, spitting a fish bone on to the ground. He gave his ragged old trousers a tug. A jellyfish slithered out of his pocket.

"The Skegglewitch? W-who's she?"

"A fiendish fluvvle," the pirate rattled. "There be no time to tell of her now. We must away to the sea, me hearty. I must be seeking *The Slippery Skeggle.*"

"*The what?*"

"My ship," the pirate beamed. "She be the finest vessel to plunder the waves." He clamped an arm round Jason's shoulder. "She be at anchor in Skegness, but I not be knowing furzackerly where. I reckon she be close to the dancing fish."

"You're crackers," said Jason. "Fish don't *dance*." They shimmied a bit, but...

The pirate seemed not to heed him. "Steer me there, shipmate. There be much adventure. You be yearning to see the sea with a seadog?"

Jason dipped a shoulder. He had to admit a few seadog adventures did sound interesting, but Mum and Dad were hardly going to let him go waltzing off with a pimply monster in a black-hooped vest that had seaweed dangling out of its trousers. So he told the pirate politely, but firmly: "No, thank you. I'm not allowed to go off with fearsome seadogs. I've got to go home for my tea. Goodbye." And he turned away sharply, praying that the pirate would run off and pester someone else.

No such luck. He had barely got into his stride when the pirate appeared in front of him again. "But shipmate, the curse."

Jason stopped walking. Oh yeah, the curse. "W-what's going to happen?"

The pirate tilted his eye to the sky. "If I be failing to find the stone, I be turned to a proper old seadog, me hearty. Doomed to stay so, for ever and a day."

Jason looked at the pirate hard. "How do you mean, a *proper* seadog?"

15

The pirate gave a broken-toothed grin. With a weak "A-haar" he twizzled around and began to turn into a mist again. The mist swirled to the ground as if it was falling through an invisible egg-timer. As it fell it steadily re-formed into...

Jason blinked and took a big step backwards. *Owp!* the dog barked. But it didn't sound like *owp!* to Jason. He distinctly heard a voice say, *This be a proper seadog, matey.*

The 'proper' seadog wagged its tail. And not for the first time that morning, there was a sniff of the seaside in the warm Midlands air.

Chapter Three

It *looked* like a scrawny, wire-haired terrier. The sort of dog that might follow a tramp. Given the choice, Jason would have happily crossed the road to avoid it. He'd seen toilet brushes in better condition.

The amazing thing was that despite the change the dog had lost none of the pirate's features. It had cracked yellow teeth and a scar down one cheek, and there were even clog-like marks on its paws. The eye patch was now just a wodge of black fur that anyone might have described as a patch, but the red-spotted scarf was exactly as before. It was knotted around the seadog's scalp and the two loose ends trailed away down his neck. It looked bizarre (on a dog at any rate) especially with pointy ears sticking up around it.

"How'd you do that?" Jason demanded. "How'd you turn yourself into a dog?"

"'Tis a toggle of the task," the seadog yapped.

"What task?"

"The task of the stone!"

"What *stone*? You said that before."

The seadog pummelled his ear with a paw. A cloud of salty gubbins flew out. "I be boggled with all these questions, boy. My head be buzzing louder than a bee. 'Tis time to weigh anchor for the side of the sea."

Jason blew a heavy sigh. He hadn't exactly banked on this, getting involved in a pirate adventure with a disgusting, talking dog. Still, it beat lying on his bed watching cobwebs form. So reluctantly he said, "Well you'd better tell me later about this stone task thing. You can't get to Skegness without me, remember."

"Fuzzlewuck," the seadog grizzled quietly.

"With knobs on," said Jason, and led the way home.

At the gate to his house on Western Avenue, he paused and said, "This is where I live. Promise you won't go and get me into trouble?"

"Cross me clogs with a cuttlefish," barked the pirate, which sounded *reasonably* trustworthy by seadog standards.

Jason dropped the latch on the gate. As he did so his attention was distracted by a sonorous voice in the garden next door. *Blaarsted greenfly*, the voice muttered

18

haughtily. It was Mrs Willoughby-Wallace. Her boat-like shape drifted out of the shadows.

Mrs 'W2', as Jason's dad liked to call her, was holding a plastic sprayer in her fist. She was jetting soapy water at the aphids on her flowers. Jason's mother had given her this gardening tip. Soap, she'd told Mrs W2, was as good at keeping greenfly at bay as it was at cleaning little boys' ears. Mrs Willoughby-Wallace had been soaping aphids with gusto ever since.

As Jason stepped further into the garden the bursts of spraying squidged to a stop. Mrs W2 had seen him. Worse than that, she had also seen the dog.

"*What* is *that?*" she demanded airily, pointing a manicured finger.

Jason gulped. The seadog was investigating the circular flower bed in the middle of the Webberly's lawn. It chewed the heads off a couple of geraniums, spat them out, then cocked its leg and weed on the stalks.

"That's – erm – Pirate," Jason explained.

"*Pirate?*"

The seadog padded over.

Mrs Willoughby-Wallace fiddled with her pearls. She wrinkled her nose as if someone had opened a bag of horse manure nearby. "Ugh," she went, "what a loathsome beast."

"Who be this fat old barrel?" yapped the dog.

"Sssshhhh!" went Jason, fearing Mrs W2 might understand the pirate's words. But Mrs Willoughby-Wallace seemed merely to hear the seadog's growl.

"Horrible, appalling animal," she hissed. And before Jason could stop her, she had lifted her sprayer and jetted some soapy water at the dog.

That was it, Jason decided, covering his eyes. Any minute now Mrs Willoughby-Wallace would be torn limb from limb and fed to a flock of passing seagulls. Yet oddly enough, the dog didn't charge. It yapped and snarled and darted about, trying to avoid the floating bubbles.

"Bubblings!" it cried. "I be under attack!"

"It's only soap," said Jason, but that just seemed to make matters worse.

The seadog howled and threw himself into a pile of old leaves. He then rolled over in some loose topsoil until his fur was totally caked with dirt.

"Disgusting creature," Mrs W2 sneered.

"Bubblewitch!" Pirate owped back angrily. He snorted loudly and a blob of phlegm shot out of his nostrils. It landed with a splat on Mrs Willougby-Wallace's shoes.

The neighbour's face turned the colour of a plum. She glowered at the dog, then at Jason. "Your mother will hear about this!" she huffed. And with a final truculent squidge of her sprayer, she waddled off towards her prize-winning roses.

Jason breathed a sigh of relief. "What'd you do that for? If you want me to show you how to get to the sea you'll have to stop growling at people first."

"She be calling me disgusting," the seadog said.

"You *are* disgusting. When was the last time you had a bath?"

"Bath?" yelped the dog as if the prospect might kill him. "I not be taking to water, boy. It be making me tidy!"

"What's wrong with that?" Fair enough, Jason didn't like a bath himself, but he wouldn't want to walk around smelling like a drain.

"It be shameful for a pirate to be tidy," said the dog.

"Well, they don't come much 'untidier' than you. You're filthy."

"Aar," went the dog, beaming like a lighthouse, "that be right swell of 'ee to say so, shipmate!"

"It wasn't meant to be a compliment," Jason sighed, but he couldn't be bothered to explain. "Now, listen. Mum doesn't like…untidy things. So you've got to behave. Otherwise, we're sunk."

"Sunk?!" The seadog sat bolt upright. "Run for the

buckets, boy! Bale out the boat!"

"Not that sort of sunk," Jason tutted. "I mean Mum won't let me take you to the seaside. You'd better go and wait round the back while I ask." He pointed the way down the side of the house. But the seadog wasn't watching. All of a sudden its nose was twitching. A trail of saliva dribbled down its chin.

"Did you understand me?" Jason frowned.

"Plain as fog on a misty day, boy. Which be the way to the galley?"

Galley? Jason repeated to himself. He stirred uneasily. Wasn't that what the kitchen on a ship was called? He opened his mouth to warn the pirate not to get up to any mischief. But the old salty seadog was already following its twitching nose – down the side of the house to the Webberly's kitchen.

Chapter Four

"I'm telling you, Brian, it was definitely on the hall shelf this morning." Mrs Webberly's voice rang out as Jason clicked the front door open and tiptoed down the hall. His parents were in the dining room. He could hear the sound of cutlery being laid out on the table. The delicious aroma of grilled fish fingers drifted along the hall from the kitchen.

"I'm telling you I haven't touched it," Mr Webberly countered, sounding narked. "Ask the kids."

Jason stopped in his tracks. "Ask the kids' usually meant 'blame Jason'. Maybe he ought to know more about this. He put his ear to the dining room door and listened.

Mrs Webberly let out a sigh. "You were the one who had it in your jacket."

Had what? Jason wondered as his dad protested,

"Shirley, that was last weekend. I've already told you, I don't know how the blooming thing got into my jacket. Kimberley must have picked it up and dropped it in my pocket. Ask her. She's the one who's been playing with it all week."

Mrs Webberly sighed again. "Kimberley, you know that perfume that came from Aunt Hester's?"

"Yes," said a tiny voice.

"Have you played with it today? Did you take it off the shelf in the hall?"

There was a scratching sound from somewhere in the kitchen. Jason ignored it and kept his ears pinned to the dining room door.

"Yes," said Kimberley.

"There," said Mr Webberly. "That's me off the hook."

Me too, Jason was thinking, when all of a sudden Kimberley added: "I put it with the bottles."

Jason froze.

"Bottles?" There was a hint of panic in Mrs Webberly's voice. "Which bottles, Kim?"

"The bottles in the *kitchen*."

"She means the ones that go to the bottle bank," her father chipped in helpfully.

At that point three things happened simultaneously: Jason's knees turned to jelly.

His mother screeched in horror.

There was a dreadful crashing sound in the kitchen.

The door to the dining room burst open. Jason's mum went sailing down the hall. She passed by so swiftly that she failed to see Jason trying to hide among the branches of a rubber plant. Jason knew he had to lie low. He had a feeling that a certain turquoise bottle was the one his mother was worried about. The one he'd treated like a hand grenade. The one that must be Aunt Hester's perfume bottle. *Perfume bottle?* Jason's jaw dropped open. But wasn't that the bottle that the seadog had—?

Before his mind could complete its workings, there was another almighty screech.

"Shirley?" Jason's dad called out. He too came lickety-split out of the dining room. He dashed into the kitchen. Jason followed at a sensible distance.

In the corner, by the cooker, the old salty seadog was standing guard over an upturned grill pan. A few fish fingers were scattered across the floor. The dog was trying to inch towards the food and was only hesitating because Jason's mum was flapping a tea towel frantically at him.

"Flamin' 'eck!" Mr Webberly exclaimed, assessing the situation with his usual dazzling turn of phrase. "Where did that thing come from?"

"The park," said Jason, rushing forward and throwing his arms around the seadog's neck.

"Don't touch it!" screamed his mother. "It might have rabies!"

"What's rabies?" said Kimberley, running in to see what the fuss was about.

"Like babies, but worse," Jason's dad explained.

"It's all right, Mum," Jason said urgently. "He's hungry and a bit scared, but he's a good dog, really. Aren't you, Pirate?" He rubbed his hand beneath the seadog's chin.

"Get your fingers out me whiskers!" the pirate barked.

Mrs Webberly frowned darkly. "Brian, do something about that dog!"

Jason's dad leapt into action. "Right. I'll...phone the RSPCA."

"I didn't mean that sort of something! This animal has just devoured our tea. Throw it out of the house, this instant!"

"I *want* the doggie," Kimberley said.

"Be quiet," said her mum. Kimberley put her fists to her eyes and wailed.

"But, Shirley, it could bite," Brian Webberly protested.

"Oh, you're hopeless," Mrs Webberly snapped, and turning to Pirate (who was snaffling a fish finger that had lodged under the fridge) she said: "Shoo!" and whacked him hard across the back with the tea towel.

"Mum, I wouldn't do that," Jason warned as the dog responded with a fearsome growl.

But now her hackles were up, Shirley Webberly wasn't the least bit frightened. "Don't you snarl at me!" she blasted. And to everyone's amazement, the seadog flattened its ears in submission and laid itself down on the kitchen floor.

That calmed the situation a little. Jason's dad breathed a sigh of relief, and Kimberley stopped crying. "Good," said Mrs Webberly, with a final petulant flick of her tea towel, "now we're getting somewhere."

The seadog rolled its eyes towards Jason. "Blistering boat-hooks," it whispered worriedly, "that wench's tongue does bite like a cat-o'-nine-tails, boy!"

Jason nodded in agreement. He knew all too well what his mum was like when she'd got a real bag on. They had to play things carefully now. "Do exactly what I say," he whispered, "or we're both for it." He stood up promptly and opened the back door. "You heard my mum. Get out, now!"

For once, the salty seadog did as it was told. It rose to its feet and slinked towards the door.

While his parents were exchanging scowls, Jason whispered in the seadog's ear. "When I shut the door, wait a little while then whimper as loudly and as sadly as you can. We've got to make Mum feel sorry for you." He shoved the dog out and banged the door to.

Mrs Webberly grabbed a kitchen roll and thrust it at her son. "Right, let's have some explanations, shall we?" She nodded at the mess on the floor.

Jason bent down and started clearing up. While he did so, he 'explained' to his mum that he'd found Pirate sniffing round the waste bins in the park.

"He was eating old banana skins and licking out yoghurt pots. I just felt sorry for him, Mum. He looked ever so hungry. I checked to see if he had a collar and everything."

Mr Webberly nodded approvingly. "Can't blame him for trying to help the dog."

Mrs Webberly seemed unmoved.

"Mummy," said Kimberley, "why has the doggie got a hankie on its head?"

"Because someone's dressed him up as a pirate," said her dad. "We'll try and find a parrot for his shoulder tomorrow – a-haar!" He closed one eye and stood on one leg. Jason started to laugh. A frosty glance from his mum put an end to that.

Kimberley tugged at her mother's skirt. "Are we keeping the pirate doggie, Mummy?"

"No," said Mrs Webberly, and pressed a button on the telephone set. Jason's heart sank as he recognised which. It was the one that held the number for the local police station. There could be only one reason why his mother was ringing the police...

"Hello," she said pertly, "I'd like to report a stray dog, please. No, it doesn't have an address tag. My son found it abandoned in the park. It's outrageously filthy and very unruly. I'm afraid you'll have to place it in strong police custody. Preferably in a good tight kennel." She smiled smugly as she said the word 'kennel'. Jason swallowed. The seadog wasn't going to like this at all. There was a pause and some tinny babble from the ear piece. Then, just as Jason was fearing the worst, the smile dissolved on his mother's face. "Your dog pen's full? *Completely* full? But...? Yes, I see..." She replaced the receiver limply. "They've had a rush on strays," she whimpered. "They want us to keep it till Tuesday."

Jason saw his chance. "Does this mean we can take Pirate to the seaside with us?"

"I'm not having that thing in the *car*," said his dad as the most awful doggie noises began to filter in through the open window.

"Mummy, the doggie's crying," said Kimberley.

Mrs Webberly covered her ears. "It sounds worse than

a cat playing a trumpet to me."

But Jason was knocking his fists together, confident now of victory. "Shall I fetch him in, Mum? Now *the police* have told us to keep him?"

"Oh, I suppose so, yes."

Jason dashed to the door and whistled the dog in. On the threshold of the kitchen he made a pretence of cuddling him.

"Unhand me, boy!" the seadog yapped. "You be worse than a barnacle on the boson's backside!"

"But you were brilliant," hissed Jason. "That's the best whimpering I've ever heard."

"Whimpering?" said Pirate looking a bit put out. "I be singing, lad! Don't you know an old salty sea shanty when you hear one?"

Chapter Five

It didn't take Mrs Webberly long to recover her composure. Once the message had begun to sink in that the seadog was there to stay a while, she immediately laid down some motherly rules.

"Number one," she told Jason, "you are wholly responsible for that *beast*. If I'm forced to lock it in the shed half the weekend, you go with it. Is that understood?"

Jason's shoulders twitched. "But Mu-um? There are spiders in the shed, what if…Pirate doesn't like them?"

"Spiders be right tasty," barked the dog. "I be liking them fondly in rum-flavoured sauce."

"Too bad," Mrs Webberly added bluntly. "If the dog gets into trouble, so do you. Rule number two: it doesn't come into the kitchen again—"

"Spit and buckets," groaned the dog, "she be worse than the cook on *The Slippery Skeggle...*"

"—and three," Mrs Webberly continued, "it's absolutely filthy. Before you go to bed tonight, I want it thoroughly hosed down."

"Seven shades o' scurvy!" the dog barked up. "That's not on!"

"BE QUIET AND SIT!" Mrs Webberly ordered it. To Jason's astonishment, the seadog sat. It was quaking gently and its ears were laid almost flat to its head. It offered Jason's mother a withering look. Jason swallowed hard. For once, he actually felt sorry for the pirate.

"Anyway," Mrs Webberly went on, "for the time being, you and this piece of wire wool on legs can run me an errand." She opened her purse and passed Jason a ten pound note. "Go and fetch us all some fish and chips."

"Aw, brilliant!" said Jason. He loved fish and chips.

"More vittles?" asked the seadog, perking up.

Mrs Webberly turned a cold eye on it. "I don't know what you think you're yapping at, dog. You've *had* all the fish anyone could eat in one night."

"I think we'd better go," Jason said hastily, nudging the dog in the direction of the hall.

The seadog gave a snort and trotted away, but it couldn't resist having a final woof at Jason's mother.

"Woof to you, too," Mrs Webberly replied.

Jason grimaced and kept his mouth shut. He didn't think his mother would like to know that in the seadog's opinion she should be dipped in tar and roped to a yardarm, preferably by her tongue, or that ten fish fingers was little more than a tasty snack to any pirate worth his weight in salt...

*

A few streets away from the Webberlys' house was a tiny fish and chip shop called *The Two-Tailed Halibut*. It was run by a man called Marios Poppalongalot, and in Jason's opinion it was the finest fish and chip shop in the whole wide world.

'Mr Poppal', as everyone knew him, was a thickset man with a shock of dark hair and a grey moustache. A pair of round, rose-tinted spectacles were always lodged on the bridge of his nose. When he wasn't wearing his fish-frying apron, silver hairs could be seen curling out of his shirt. He wore rings on four fingers and his ears were pierced. He walked with a gentle limp.

Mr Poppal hadn't owned the *Halibut* for long, but he was already a firm favourite with the Webberly family. He always gave them generous portions of chips. Or a free tub of peas. Or a saveloy, perhaps. Sometimes Jason saw the old man driving down to the market for fish. He

31

was easy to spot in his yellow Beetle car. As he chugged past, Jason would throw him a wave and Mr Poppal would pip his horn in return. A friendly pip seemed to sum Mr Poppal up. He was a pleasant, happy, carefree man who had a kind word for everyone. He also liked to greet his customers in style.

"Jase! My boy. Come in. Come in-nn. So good to see you again!"

Mr Poppal's rich Mediterranean tones sliced through the steam and the sizzle of oil. He gave a wide-mouthed grin and flapped a piece of unbattered cod at his visitors.

The seadog growled and bared his teeth. "Who be this wobbling walrus, boy?"

"Pack it in," warned Jason. "Mr Poppal's my friend. He doesn't allow dogs in his shop. *You* have to wait outside and be quiet."

"But there be salt in there, boy," the seadog hissed.

"So?" said Jason. "What's the big deal about—?"

Before he could complete his sentence, the dog had bowled in and plonked his paws on the bright silver counter. "STAND BY TO BE BOARDED!" he barked.

Jason immediately tried to shoo him out. But Mr Poppal was as calm as a baked potato. He picked up a cleaning cloth and waggled it under the seadog's nose.

"Blistering barnacles!" the pirate cried. He reeled

back sharply and scuttled away to a corner of the shop.

Mr Poppal wiped the paw marks off the counter. He patted the cloth as if it held some sort of magical power. Jason leaned forward and sniffed it. The fabric bore a strong scent of pine disinfectant.

"Too sharp," said Mr Poppal, tapping his nose. "He not like it much."

"It's bubblings," said Jason. "He's frightened of soap."

Mr Poppal nodded sagely. He flicked an owl-keen glance at the seadog. "Strange kinda doggie, ain't he, Jase? Looks like he came off a pirate ship."

"That's what I call him – Pirate," said Jason. "I found him in the park. I'm sorry he jumped up. I think he's hungry."

Mr Poppal gave an understanding nod. "Tell you what. Old Poppa has scraps in the back. Stuff no good for you and me. But a doggie like Pirate, he eat this up. I get it for him. You wait there."

Mr Poppal retreated through a doorway covered by multi-coloured plastic strips. He returned a few moments later carrying what looked like a washing-up bowl. Heaped in the bowl were the most foul-looking scraps Jason had ever seen: smelly fish-heads, rotting tomatoes, manky bits of lettuce, mouldy old sausages. It looked like Mr Poppal had raided the bins.

Jason said, "I don't think he'll want *that*."

But the seadog smacked his lips and whined. He got even more excited when Mr Poppal picked up the salt shaker.

"Yes? No?"

The seadog barked.

"I think he'd like some," Jason said.

Mr Poppal shook the salt. The dog barked again.

"Bit more," Jason said with a grimace.

The dog barked again.

"More?" asked Mr Poppal, who didn't appear remotely surprised at the amount of salt the dog seemed to want.

Jason winced. "He likes a bit of seasoning with his food, Mr Poppal."

While the seadog was wolfing down the scraps, Mr Poppal served Jason with the family's fish and chips. He enquired, casually, what the Webberly clan was up to that weekend.

"We're supposed to be going to Skegness," Jason muttered.

Mr Poppal raised an eyebrow. He seemed interested, but not wholly surprised. "You taking the dog?"

Jason bit his lip. He wasn't really sure. Now that the 'perfume' bottle was smashed, there was no real reason to go to Skegness. But that would leave several questions unanswered, and top of the list was this: why did Aunt Hester have a perfume bottle with an old salty seadog stoppered inside it?

"Hey," said Mr Poppal, shaking Jason's arm. "One penny for your thoughts, my friend?"

Jason blinked and shook his head slightly. "Sorry, I was thinking about Aunt Hester."

Mr Poppal seemed to suck in sharply. "You tell me about her before, I think. She the old woman who live on the sea front, in the house called Shingle Towers?"

"Yes, you've got a good memory."

Mr Poppal gave a tight-lipped grin. Jason wasn't sure but he thought he could see a little anxiety in the chip shop owner's normally placid features. But at that moment, another customer entered the shop and Mr Poppal became his jolly self again. "Goodbye, my friend. You have a nice weekend. You take care with that doggie, hey?"

Jason nodded and waved goodbye.

But on the short walk back to Western Avenue, he thought hard about what Mr Poppal had said: *You take care with Pirate.* Why did he get the oddest feeling Mr Poppal was trying to warn him about something? Jason glanced uneasily at the dog. How come it could eat a whole shaker of salt without yakking up at the first swallow? It hadn't even wanted a drink. "Drat," Jason muttered as the thought of a drink suddenly jerked his memory awake: he'd forgotten the ginger beer. Ordering Pirate to 'stay' (the dog at this moment was keeling against a lamp-post anyway) he hurried back to *The Two-Tailed Halibut*. He could not have been away for more than a minute. Yet, to his surprise, the lights were off and a sign was on the door.

**Due to circumstances beyond control
– forced to close for weekend.**

Jason frowned and backed away – unaware that from an upstairs room, Mr Poppalongalot was watching him carefully.

Chapter Six

Over tea, all the talk was of Great-Aunt Hester.

"Poor dear," Mrs Webberly murmured, "it's going to be awful – breaking the news."

"It was only a bit of pong," said Mr Webberly, sprinkling vinegar on his fish.

Jason nearly choked on a mouthful of orange juice.

"Drink slower," said his mother and turned back to her husband. "That's not the point, Brian. Some things have great sentimental value. Hester was quite upset about that bottle. She told me on the phone it's very special. It's been in her family for three hundred years. I expect it must be some sort of heirloom. She'll be heartbroken to know it's gone. What makes it doubly worse is that it's one of a set."

"Uh?" went Jason, letting his fork slip out of his grasp.

It clattered onto the table top. *Set?* Had his mother just said *set?* So there were *more* bottles? Did that mean…more pirates? Suddenly he felt like turning to jelly and slithering away into a corner of the room.

"If you want to ask a question, say 'pardon'," said his mum. "'Uh' is for cavemen. We've come on a bit since then."

"S-sorry," Jason stuttered.

"Uh," said Kimberley.

"Well?" asked Mrs Webberly impatiently. "What was it you wanted to ask?"

Jason wasn't entirely sure. His mind was filling up with creepy thoughts, most of them to do with Great Aunt Hester. Did she know there was a pirate in her perfume bottle? If she didn't, someone really ought to tell her. Then again, maybe she knew about the seadog and didn't want anyone else to find out. Maybe what she'd said to Mum on the phone was really just a ruse to put her off the scent (so to speak). Maybe she was hiding a deep, dark secret?

And it was then that an idea prodded Jason's mind. An idea so frightening that his mouth fell open and a half-chewed pea came tumbling out. What if Aunt Hester not only knew what the bottles contained, but had filled them up herself?

What if she was…the *Skegglewitch?*

Jason thought this through very carefully. Aunt Hester, a witch? Could it really be possible? On hag-like looks she qualified, no problem. She had a nose as long as a penguin's beak and teeth as crooked as lighthouse steps. She hobbled around on a gnarled old stick that could have been a tree branch scorched by lightning. And what about the hairy warts on her elbows? And the horrible yellowing in the 'whites' of her eyes? And the veins on her legs that stood out like worms? And—

"Well?" Mrs Webberly tapped the table top.

"Uh?" went Jason, jumping in his seat.

"Oh do stop *grunting*. I thought you were going to ask me something?"

Jason swallowed a piece of fish. He could hardly ask his mum if Aunt Hester was a witch. And yet the proof of it was fast asleep in the hall, snoring like a drain and letting off gruesome eggy smells. But what could he say that would make her believe him? *When I smashed the bottle, Mum, a pirate came out.* It sounded crackers. Jason clenched a fist in frustration. No, he couldn't tell his mum just yet. He needed more evidence. Concrete proof. So he did ask a very tentative question: How many bottles were in the set?

"I'm not entirely sure," Mrs Webberly replied, cutting

Kimberley's fish into squares, "I got the impression there were quite a few."

Quite a few? A whole *crew*, perhaps? Jason lowered his knife. "Where does she keep them?"

Mrs Webberly's eyebrows locked into a frown. "It's funny you should ask me that; Hester only mentioned it herself this morning. Apparently, she keeps them in the cellar."

Jason felt his spine turn rigid. The pirates were imprisoned in bottles, in the *cellar*?

"I agree, it's odd," Mrs Webberly said, catching his slightly startled expression. "Perhaps she feels they're safe down there. Or they keep better in the cold, like wine."

"Perhaps she's got the two mixed up," said Mr Webberly. "Perhaps she dabs plonk behind her ears in the morning and swigs a glass of pong before bed every night. She's as nutty as a fruitcake. She's definitely going senile."

"I *like* sea lions," Kimberley said, swinging her pigtails back and forth. One caught in a blob of tomato sauce, causing her mother to cluck like a hen.

Mr Webberly leaned a little closer to his son. "Bet I know the *real* reason. The bottles would be nice and handy in the cellar. When she wakes up in the dead of night and pushes back her coffin lid, there's the perfume collection right next to the glass of bat's blood with her false fangs in it and—"

"Do you mind?" Mrs Webberly cut in, wiping Kimberley's hair with a tissue. "This is my relation we're talking about."

"Oh, come on," Mr Webberly laughed. "You have to admit she is a bit spooky. Anyway, we're not entirely sure she *is* your relation."

Jason switched his gaze to his mum. "Who is she, then?"

Mrs Webberly turned Kimberley's plate around to avoid a repeat of the tomato sauce incident. "Jason, don't talk about your aunt as if she's some sort of 'thing'. She's a very remarkable lady. She was easily in her sixties when I met her as a girl – and look at her now, still going strong. She was my grandmother's second cousin twice removed – we think. The family records are rather vague, but her blood is in our veins all right."

"I don't want her blood in my veins!" Jason shouted. He put down his cutlery and batted his arms.

"We could suck it out with leeches?" Mr Webberly suggested.

"What's leeches?" asked Kimberley.

"Oh, like peaches, but not as sweet," said her mum,

flashing her husband a rather stern look. "Now, eat your tea. And Jason, will you please stop jigging about? I admit Aunt Hester is a little…eccentric, but her heart's, well, in the right place."

Hmph, thought Jason, stabbing at a chip, bet she keeps her *heart* in the cellar as well. Packed away in a box of ice. He frowned and had a drink of juice. This whole situation was worse than he'd imagined. Why had Aunt Hester got a whole pirate crew imprisoned in her cellar? What had they done to get put into bottles?

"What's eggsentrick?" Kimberley asked.

"It means silly," said her dad.

"Creepy," added Jason, having another bout of the shivers.

"Creepy?" Kimberley looked sideways at her mum, and in so doing managed to push a chip into her ear rather than her open mouth.

Mrs Webberly sighed in defeat and set about Kimberley's ear with a tissue. "Don't you listen to these two," she whispered. "They're only jealous because the women in our family have always been a bit special."

"Special?" gulped Jason. "How do you mean?"

Mrs Webberly raised her eyebrows to the limit. "Well, take your Aunt June, for instance. She was a dab hand at predicting the weather. All she needed was a snail and an old piece of seaweed – and a jam-jar if a storm was expected. She used to stick it to her ear and listen for thunder. Amazingly accurate she was. And Grandma could read the leaves, of course."

"Tea leaves?"

Mrs Webberly shook her head. "No, just leaves as they fluttered off the trees. She once told your grandad the precise result of a football match, purely by counting the leaves that fell on one side of the garden against the leaves that fell on the other."

"It was a great match," Mr Webberly put in. "Leicester won 349 to 348, they got the winning leaf in injury time."

Mrs Webberly gave her husband a very hard stare. "You can mock," she said. "But I'm telling you, my family have the gift."

"The gift for being bonkers," Mr Webberly sniffed. "And they're faddy, too." He picked up a slice of lemon from his plate. "I mean, why is it that whenever we have tea at Aunt Hester's house we're not allowed to have any vinegar with our chips or a squirt of lemon on our fish? What's wrong with a squirt of lemon for goodness' sake?"

Mr Webberly squeezed his lemon and sent a jet of juice down Jason's sweatshirt.

"Aw, Da-ad?!"

Mrs Webberly slowly fumed. "Perhaps she doesn't want drowning in lemon juice!"

Jason dabbed at the splash with his sleeve. This was hopeless. It was time to get matters back on track. "What time are we going to Skegness tomorrow?"

His father answered that. "Personally, I can't see the point in us driving out to Skeg for the pleasure of getting our heads bitten off. Aunt Hester's sure to blow a gasket when she finds out what's happened to that bottle."

"But you promised we could take Pirate to the seaside!"

"We never promised anything," Mrs Webberly said, unruffled. "And put that top in the wash basket, please, before you go for your bath."

Jason buried his face in his hands.

"Jason, stop sulking," Mrs Webberly tutted. "As it happens I think we *should* go back to Skegness tomorrow. I intend to buy Hester a new bottle of perfume. Not much of a replacement for a family heirloom, but giving her a gift is the least I can do."

Mr Webberly's suggestion was somewhat more radical. "I'd send a letter and leave the country."

"You would. You quake if she as much as looks at you. No, it's no good taking the evasive option. I made the mistake. I ought to apologise to Hester in person. If she's angry, she's angry. These things have to be faced."

"Mum," said Jason, suddenly feeling worried at the thought of his mum facing up to a Skegglewitch, "you will be careful with Aunt Hester, won't you?"

Mrs Webberly eyed him strangely. "What's that supposed to mean?"

"It means he agrees with me," said his dad. "When the old witch discovers you've scuppered her pong she's probably going to turn you into a crab."

"That's not funny," Jason said, getting down noisily from the table.

Mr Webberly opened his arms. "What did I say?"

His wife just sighed and shook her head.

"I *like* crabs," Kimberley announced.

47

Chapter Seven

By quarter to nine, Jason had been for his hair wash and bath. He was in his pyjamas, getting ready for bed, when the bedroom door opened and the old salty seadog trotted in.

"Take it. It's driving us mad," said his mother. "I can hardly hear the telly for the sound of its snoring."

The seadog belched and hopped onto the bed. "Aar, this be a snugglesome berth."

Mrs Webberly gave it a frosty glare. "Tuesday," she said. And out she went.

"Right," said Jason, as the dog settled into a fold of the duvet, "I want some answers from you."

"I be right snuzzly," the seadog yawned. "I not be in a yarning mood."

Jason grabbed him by the snout. "If you don't tell me

how you got into that bottle I'll make myself sick. Then we won't go to Skegness tomorrow and you'll stay a dog for *ever*. Woof! Woof!"

The seadog twizzled an ear in submission. Jason released his grip. He climbed into bed and nudged the dog hard with his foot.

"It be shrivelsome sorcery," the seadog barked. "I be squeezed to the size of a scorpion's squint, dangled by the britches and dropped in. Plop!"

"By Aunt Hester? Did she cast a spell on you?"

"Hester? What be a Hester, boy?"

"Our crabby old relation who lives in Skegness."

"A fine old town," the seadog said. "There be many a good crab there, me hearty."

"Never mind the crabs," Jason tutted. "Is Aunt Hester the *Skegglewitch*?"

At the mention of the Skegglewitch the seadog took a much keener interest. "Be she having an evil countenance, lad? Eyes like the moon and hair the colour of a toasted turnip?"

"Well," said Jason, having to think, "she's got horn-rimmed specs and a purple rinse. She lives in a house called Shingle Towers."

"That be her!" the seadog barked. "She be a scutterbuck, shipmate! A bent old crone! A hideous rag with a fire-spitting tongue!"

"I knew it," said Jason, tightening his fist. "I knew there was something fishy about her."

"Aye," said the dog. "She be right fishy. She be scales and weed and wussely bits."

"Wussely bits?" Jason screwed up his nose. "She didn't look "wussely" when I saw her last week. Or weedy. Or scaly. Are you telling me fibs?"

"Nay," yapped the dog. "The Skegglewitch be a fiendish fluvvle. I do swear on the hairs of a dead man's vest."

"Hmm," went Jason. Swearing on the hairs of a dead man's vest was a new one to him, but it sounded pretty fair by seadog standards. "So why did she do it – bottle you, I mean? Is it something to do with that stone you were on about?"

The seadog pricked his ears. "You know of the saltstone, lad?"

Jason shook his head. "Saltstone? What's that?" In his mind's eye he pictured a shining jewel encrusted in seashells and sitting in the mouth of a giant clam.

The pirate's description was no less poetic. "'Tis a wondrous briny charm," he barked, a wet tongue lolling out of his mouth. "The most lickable treasure in the seven seas, aar."

Lickable? Jason grimaced slightly and wiped some

doggy slobber off his duvet. Who would want to lick a stone? Especially a *salty* one. Yuk. "Why are you always going on about salt? Why do you eat so much of it?"

The seadog tightened his claws a little. "'Tis a bane of the witch's potion," he grizzled. "A terrible tale of trickerous treachery. Should I be telling 'ee now of our piratey quest?"

Jason raised a half-interested eyebrow.

The seadog leaned a little closer and whispered, "One night we be at anchor off the shores of Skegness, when the witch be puffling out of a fog."

Jason shuddered and rubbed his arms. "Scary. What did she want?"

"To be bartering, shipmate. To be making a trade. She be hearing that we be a fine band of men and wanting us to fare on a grand adventure."

"To find the saltstone, you mean?"

The seadog nodded. "She be pledging many chests of sparklesome treasure if the crew be sailing to Grubblemuck Island and bringing the wondrous gobbet ashore. The stone be deep in a craggly cave. It be guarded by quaggle ducks and nine-headed newts. Aar, 'twas a most ticklish skirmish. I nearly be losing my nose to a gobbler fish."

Jason shuddered again. Gobbler fish? He thought he'd

heard of them. He took the subject back to salt. "What about this potion? Where does that come in?"

The seadog ground what teeth he possessed. "That be the trickerous part," he growled. "The night afore we set sail on our quest, the crew be making merry at Shingle Towers. The witch be serving rum and vittles. We be greatly gogglesome, lad. I not be right steady on my clogs that night. As the moon be growing bigly and round, the witch be appearing with a steaming brew. She be saying it be a guard against ogres. We be crying *a-haar!* and quaffling the draught. 'Twas a most grievous toast. From that day for'ard the crew be having a strange, uncommon taste for salt. We be chewing our britches to find a bibble."

Flipping heck, thought Jason, who didn't fancy chewing *his* britches for anything. "So she'd cast a spell on the potion that would make you really thirsty for salt – just to make sure you'd carry out your quest?"

"That be the bones of it," the seadog said.

"She'd made you a sort of...salt pirate?"

"Aye," said the dog. "She be a trufferous toad."

"But what did she want the saltstone for? What use is a salty stone to her?"

"I not be furzackerly knowing," said the dog.

"Spells," muttered Jason, gritting his teeth. "I bet she

wants it for wicked spells."

The seadog nodded. "'Tis a likely prospect."

"And you gave it to her?"

The dog shook his head. "Nay, shipmate. The crew be right enticed with the gobbet. There be much gruffling about the trade. Mr Scabb be saying we should hold the stone and sail to the far-off corners of the world. Mr Blue Thumb, he be agreeing with him."

"Mr Scabb and Mr Blue Thumb? Are they part of your crew?"

"Fearsome seadogs both, a-haar!"

Jason grimaced. Mr Scabb sounded hideous. "Go on. What happened next?"

"Cap'n Blackhead be stabbing his cutlass in the mast and saying he have the rightest notion."

"Captain BLACKHEAD?!"

A voice bellowed up from the lounge below. "Jason Webberly, get to sleep."

"Blackhead?" Jason repeated in a whisper.

The seadog nodded proudly. "The cap'n be as foul as fungus, boy; a fine example to pirating men. He be stirring up a cunning plan. He be breaking off a tiny niblet of the stone and saying we be taking that morsel to the witch."

Jason looked puzzled. "What's the point of that?"

"To cross the witch and play for more treasure!"

Jason slapped a hand across his brow. "That's not cunning. That's just dumb. No one crosses a witch."

"Aye, 'twas a wretched venture," sighed the dog. He flattened his mangy ears and a sorrowful look came into his eyes. "As soon as we be dropping anchor, the cap'n and the crew be taking arms and stealing away to Shingle Towers, there to be bartering with the witch. I be left aboard *The Skeggle* with the prisoner and the parrot."

"Prisoner?" Jason squashed a pillow into his lap. The dog had never mentioned a prisoner before.

The pirate nodded. "Aye, on our passage to Grubblemuck Island a trading ship be crossing our bows. We be sinking it fair and taking a captive. He be right noble and jaunty."

"Where is he? Did the Skegglewitch get him?"

The seadog cocked his head in thought. "I not be rightly knowing, boy."

Jason sighed in frustration. Another mystery. "OK, what happened to the parrot?"

The seadog did have an answer for this. "Bottled," he said, his tone rather flat.

"How?" said Jason. "I thought you were on guard."

"That be true. But the Skegglewitch be right fearful, boy. She be puffling up in a terrible storm. The boat be rocking from side to side. There be water lashing over the gunnels. I never be seeing a sea so rageful. The witch be spitting cockles and goo. She be saying Cap'n Blackhead be a double-eyed dogfish and the crew but a heap of mongering warts. Their treachery be rewarded, she said, *by a taste of her skeggling curse.*"

"She'd shrunk them, you mean?"

"Shrimped, to a man. She be saying they be stowed in a bag full of fleas in a cold dark hole in Shingle Towers."

"Ugh," went Jason scratching his arms.

"She be telling me I be joining them, boy, lest I be giving up the most of the stone."

Great choice, thought Jason. "What did you do?"

The seadog quaked in his clog-like patches. "I be doing my best to parley. I be saying if the witch be lifting her spell, I be showing where the stone be hid."

"That was brave. Where *was* it hid?"

The seadog drew his shoulders in. "Deep in the belly of a blistering cannon."

"A CANNON?!"

"'Twas Mr Floggem's notion! He be in charge of hidings – and floggings."

Jason shuddered. Mr Floggem sounded even more grisly than the others. "But what if someone had lit the fuse?"

The seadog gritted his teeth and grimaced.

"Oh no," gasped Jason. "You didn't fire the

saltstone *out of the cannon?*"

"'Twas an accident, boy! 'Twas dark on deck. The parrot be squawking high in the rigging. I be slipping on one of its cowardly droppings. My lantern be wibbling about the fuse and POOM! the stone be flying seaward."

"But the Skegglewitch…she must have gone crackers?"

The seadog gave a tremulous gulp. "Aye. The witch be narked as a noggin."

I'm not surprised, thought Jason. Narked as a noggin barely seemed to do it justice. "Is that when she shrank you?"

The seadog sniffed. "She be pointing a wussely finger and *poof!* I be shrivelled to the measure of a piffling biscuit. She be taking a bottle from her witchly pouch and…"

"Plop. Dropped you in it…" Jason gulped.

"Aye," the dog lamented quietly. "Tombed in glass, for ever and a day…"

Chapter Eight

"But you're not." Jason drew up the covers and touched them gently against his mouth. "You're not in your bottle. You're here, on my bed. Something must have changed."

The seadog twizzled his snout. He looked right and left (and once at Jason's teddy as if that might be a spy) then leaned forward and whispered, "There be rumblings, shipmate."

Jason looked a bit put out. "Well go to the loo if your tummy's not right."

The seadog burped and shook his head. "Nay, lad. Not tumbly rumblings. There be news on the tide that the gobbet be ashore."

"But you just said you fired it out to sea."

"Aye, but the witch be reporting it found. One day, she be bringing my bottle from the hole and resting it on her wussely palm. I be seeing her bigly through the glass. She be cackling at me, clear as a pebble. She be telling me three hundred years be passed and now be the time I be paying for my meddlings. I be sent on a piratey task, she said, to recover that part of the stone I once be blasting o'er the waves."

"That's it, then? That's your task? Find the stone and take it to her?"

The seadog gave a quiet nod.

"But how will you know where to look for it?"

"Aar," grinned the dog. "I be having a map. It be nestling nicely neath my kerchief."

Jason slid his hand under the seadog's scarf. Sure enough, he found a crumpled piece of parchment. He opened it out on the bed.

"It shows the way from Shingle Towers all the way to Skegness." He pointed to a useless drawing of a house and an even worse one of the clock tower at the centre of the town. Joining the drawings were two straight lines with a dashed line down the middle (the old sea road, Jason guessed). To the right of these lines was a jumble of dots (sand). Further right still were some wavy lines (the sea). That part of the map was easy to understand. But several things did puzzle Jason. First, in the region that was meant to be sand were a lot of doggy paw

marks. They stretched the entire length of the beach, ending at Shingle Towers. Also, at the top of the map, was a large but simple outline of a fish. It was standing upright on its tail, as if it was swimming north. A slightly wavy box had been drawn around it. A vertical line from the box connected the fish to another drawing: of a pirate ship. The centre of the ship was marked with a cross. Jason plonked a finger on it.

Panting lightly the seadog said, "The stone be at the sign of the dancing fish."

Jason glanced at the fish again. There were curve marks around its tail – as if it might be dancing. "What about this boat?"

"I reckon that be *The Slippery Skeggle*."

Jason looked a bit uncertain. "I've been to Skegness loads of times. I've never seen a pirate ship."

"It be a fine old boat," the seadog yapped, "all a-bar the figurehead, aar. That be toggling seaward when we be ramming the prisoner's boat."

Jason shuddered and plumped the pillow. The less swashbuckling antics he heard about the better. He quickly changed tack. "OK, so you've got a map and we know your task, but there's still one thing you haven't told me: why can you turn into a dog?"

The seadog clamped his teeth in embarrassment. "I be

toggled by the witch. 'Tis a terrible blight. If Cap'n Blackhead be knowing, I be sorrowful shamed."

"But why's she done it? She must have a reason?"

The seadog lifted a mangy shoulder. "When she be bringing my bottle from the hole I be begging for mercy and saying I be nought but a poor old seadog. The witch be rubbing her warty chin, then be gleeful cackling again. She be pointing at my bottle and *poosh!* I be turned to a mangy cur. *Double poosh!* I be a pirate once more. 'There,' she be hissing, '*now* you can be a SEADOG at will. Use this skill to sniff out the stone and bring it here, to Shingle Towers. Fail me and you stay a four-legged fool for ever.'"

"Tough task," whistled Jason.

"Aar," growled the dog. "But I be having my revenge most bigly, shipmate. I be furnishing a cunning plan."

Jason's shoulders turned a little cold. He didn't like the idea of the pirate having 'plans'.

"I be crossing the Skegglewitch, lad – avenging my shipmates, one and all. I be taking this map and finding *The Skeggle*. Then I be sailing to the witch's lair and opening fire with cannon. I be freeing the cap'n and crew from their bottles. Then we be doing for the witch. A-haar!"

Jason blew a scornful bubble. There were more holes

in this 'plan' than you'd find in a cheese grater. "You can't sail a ship single-handed," he said. "And if you blast the house, you'll blow up your crew. Anyway, if you don't hand over the stone, you'll be chasing cats for the rest of your life."

The seadog gave a grizzling sniff. "I not be thinking on that," he admitted.

Jason rolled his eyes. "What you ought to do is this: sneak into the Skegglewitch's cellar first, make off with the bottles, release the crew, *then* go and find *The Slippery Skeggle*. Then you can all sail back to Shingle Towers and tell the Skegglewitch to break her spell or get blown to smithereens."

The dog leapt up in excitement. "Cod 'n' bones! That be considerable cunning!"

"Shush," hissed Jason, hearing movement in the lounge. "You'll bring Mum up."

The seadog lowered his voice. "How be we making off with the bottles?"

"Easy," Jason whispered, leaning forward. "The key to the cellar is – hang on. *I'm* not in on this."

"But shipmate," the pirate pleaded doggily, standing up on all fours now. "You be saving the bones of a fine band of men. You be goodly rewarded. A handsome treasure chest be yours for the asking."

"Yeah, well," Jason muttered, beginning to feel just a touch heroic. Now his conscience was going through hoops. The seadog had a point. This was a battle of good against evil (well, semi-bad against evil). So should he do the *honourable* thing and help the seadog battle Aunt Hester? Or should he do the *sensible* thing and forget all about it? He flicked the pirate a sympathetic glance. Devious and untrustworthy as he probably was, Jason felt an odd camaraderie with him. In the end, basic goodness tipped the balance.

"All right, I'll help you get the bottles. But there'd better not be any plundering and stuff."

"Plundering?" said the dog, a picture of innocence.

"I know about pirates," Jason said. "They're brigands and cut-throats. There'd better not be any marauding or despoiling. I'm always in trouble with Mum as it is."

The seadog had a careful think. "Be we taking the mumly wench with us, boy? Set her walking a bendy plank?"

"Not likely!"

"Be we putting her in a barrel and throwing her overboard?"

"No. You promise not to hurt her. Or Dad."

"What be we doing with the little piece of whalebait?"

"Or Kimberley. Promise *now*."

"Promise what?" Suddenly the bedroom door creaked open. "Hmm," went Mrs Webberly, hands on her hips. Jason had his eyes closed, head on the pillow. The old salty seadog was curled into a ball. "No more noise, you two, all right?" Mrs Webberly crossed the room and drew the curtains. "You fast asleep there, Jason?"

"Yes, Mum," he said, screwing up his face the instant he'd said it. Why did he fall for that one every time?

Mrs Webberly grinned. "Night, night," she said. The bedroom door closed with a clunk.

"Pirate, are *you* still awake?" whispered Jason.

Snoring sounds rose from the bottom of the bed.

And this time, they were the real thing.

Chapter Nine

Jason hated the drive to Skegness. It was nothing but
miles of country roads and flat fields full of sprouts and
cabbages. The 'scenic route' his parents called it. The
'seen it' route was how Jason described it. When you'd
seen one cabbage, you'd seen them all. And there were
lots of cabbages between Leicester and Skegness.

But that morning he was glad of the lengthy ride.
Daring plans were much in his mind and he needed the
time to think them through. Top of the list was his plan to
break into Aunt Hester's cellar. He had plotted the details
during breakfast and was checking them now for possible
snags. The cellar door was kept permanently locked – no
problem, he knew where the key was hidden: in a biscuit
tin at the top of the pantry. Stealing it would be easier
than picking his nose. On a given cue, the seadog would

whimper and Jason would offer to take him for a walk. His mother would say yes, glad enough to have them both out of mischief. He and Pirate would go out through the kitchen. Then, while the dog kept a careful lookout, Jason would climb on to a stool and grab the key. When the coast was clear, they would double back down the long, tiled hall and sneak quietly into the cellar. Easy-peasy. A piece of cake. They would have the bottles out in a jiffy. The craggy old Skegglewitch wouldn't suspect a thing.

Yet, something niggled him about the plan. Pirates were pirates, after all. Who was going to thank him for freeing them? He couldn't see himself being knighted by the Queen or thanked by the Prime Minister for setting a band of cut-throats loose. And what were the pirates going to do with the stone? What if they used its power for plundering? The car eased round a set of roadworks. 'SKEGNESS – 10 MILES' a large sign said. Jason frowned. He needed answers. In another half hour, battle would commence.

But it was difficult talking to the dog in the car. Kimberley had commandeered him for a start. She'd been prattling away non-stop to the pirate ever since Dad had closed the garage doors. The pirate was lying flopped out on his tummy. His snout was buried in the crook of his paws and his ears were laid flatter than the surface of a mirror. This was no defence against Kimberley. Every now and then she would poke him with a pencil and the seadog would be forced to raise his head. Jason felt for him. He really did. Especially when Kimberley got out her pad and began to draw her stupid pictures.

"This is our garden," she said, doing a scribble. She pointed at the tangle of lines on the paper. "Here's Mummy hanging out the washing. And here's Daddy mowing the lawn. And here's our apple tree. And here's Jason, behind it – scratching his bottom."

"Where?" said Jason, craning his neck to examine the sprawling, criss-crossing lines. No matter how often he looked at Kimberley's pictures, he only ever saw a ball of wool.

"Go away," said Kimberley, "I'm playing with the doggie."

"The doggie's bored out of his brain," said Jason.

"Aye, 'tis a dreadful passage," said the pirate, letting out an exhausted whimper.

Mrs Webberly beamed over her shoulder. "Everybody all right in the back?"

"NO!" barked Jason and the seadog together.

"Nearly there," said Mr Webberly, "just round the next bend."

Jason groaned and pulled his knees up to his chest.

There were a million bends between Leicester and Skegness. His father said that at half of them at least.

"Let's play a game," Mrs Webberly said. "'Name Ten Things' - we all like that."

"Good idea," said her husband. "I'll start, shall I? Name ten things on…"

"A pirate ship," Jason muttered half-heartedly, thinking at that moment of *The Slippery Skeggle*. Were they really going to find a pirate boat in Skegness? Why hadn't he seen it there before?

"A pirate ship?" His mother groaned. "Oh, all right, if it'll keep you happy. The first thing I see is…a skull and crossbones."

"For'ard or aft?" the seadog yapped. It jumped up suddenly and plonked its paws on the front two seats. "Batten down the hatches, boy! Bite on your cutlass!"

"Get down!" said Mrs Webberly, shoving the dog back.

Jason gave the seadog's headscarf a tug. "Cool it," he whispered, "it's only a game. You have to name ten things you'd see on your ship."

"The gizzards of a gribbling gull!" barked the seadog. "Nine crates of rum! A spider's spit! A mouldy tub of lard! A salted whalebone! A—"

"Will you be QUIET?!" Mrs Webberly whipped round and gave the seadog an icy glare. "Any more yapping and we shall stop this car and ditch you in the nearest field, MUTT."

"MUTTINY!" barked the seadog. "Cast adrift!"

"Sssh." Jason threw his arm round Pirate and wrestled him flat to the seat again. "I think he's just excited, Mum. He can probably smell the seaside air."

This was a reasonable explanation. In the last few minutes the unmistakeable aroma of sand and seaweed and fresh salt air had been wafting in through the vents of the car. Nevertheless, Mrs Webberly was not impressed.

"I'll give it 'seaside'," she muttered darkly. "Now listen, Jason, I've something to tell you. When we get to Aunt Hester's, I want you to—"

"Pirates," Kimberley interrupted suddenly.

Mrs Webberly frowned. "What about them?"

"*That's* what you'd see on a piratey ship."

"Well done, Kim," her father laughed.

Mrs Webberly sighed. "Kim, we're not playing the game any more. Put your pad away. We'll be there in a minute."

Kimberley bit the end of her pencil. "I've drawed a picture of the doggie," she whispered, and turned it round for her mother to see.

"Delightful," said her mother, as graciously as she could.

"How be this likeness?" the seadog yapped. "Do I be shown in a kindly light?"

Jason leaned over and had a look. All he could see was yet more wool. "Where?" he asked. "I can't see a dog."

"You can't *see* him, silly. He's in his *kennel*."

The seadog whimpered and gnawed at the seat. Jason said something very unbrotherly and pulled his sweatshirt over his head.

"As I was saying," Mrs Webberly continued, yanking the sweatshirt down again. "When we get to Aunt Hester's I want you and this ragbag to disappear for a while."

"Yes, Mum," Jason muttered – then checked himself. No, that wasn't part of the plan. If he was shut out of Shingle Towers he couldn't sneak around and get the key to the cellar. "But, don't you want me to say hello to her, Mum? Don't you want me to…give her a kiss?" That made him really quiver. He couldn't believe he'd actually said that. Kissing Aunt Hester was like putting your lips on a pair of wriggling caterpillars. Honestly, the things a hero was expected to do.

"Kiss her?" Mrs Webberly gave Jason a doubtful stare. "Are you feeling all right? You've always treated Hester like a radioactive alien in the past."

"What's an aly-men?" asked Kimberley.

"A green thing with four eyes that grunts," said her dad.

"I know this beast," the seadog yapped. "It be hiding

in a hole on Grubblemuck Island."

"Sure," scoffed Jason.

"Don't talk back," his mother scolded. "Now, as soon as we get there, take the dog to the beach or something. Let it chase a stick. With any luck it'll keep on running and won't come back."

Before Jason could protest any further, the car braked sharply and everyone tilted forward in their seats.

"'Tis a wayward westerly wind," barked the dog.

Mr Webberly frowned in apology. "It's this flipping yellow Beetle. It's been on my tail all the way to Skegness. It's finally decided to overtake me. There it goes, look, off towards the sea front. If I didn't know better, I'd say it was Mr Poppal's."

Jason looked up. There was indeed a yellow Beetle car in the distance. It was accelerating away so fast he let himself imagine that it might be robbers in a getaway vehicle. But what if his dad was right? What if it wasn't a robber at all, but an old Greek man with rose-coloured specs and a fish-frying apron?

Jason shook his head. That didn't make sense.

After all, what would Mr Poppal be doing out here?

Chapter Ten

Although Aunt Hester's house was on the sea front, Mr Webberly had to drive through the centre of Skegness to get there. Jason liked this part of the journey. At first glance, Skegness was a town like any other. All the familiar stores were there, bustling with the usual Saturday shoppers. But as the car nudged closer to the edge of the land and eventually turned parallel to the sea itself, everything changed. The shops here were bursting with picture postcards, silly hats, T-shirts, cheap mirrored sunglasses, buckets, spades, frisbees, towels, windmills, flip-flops, pennants, multicoloured footballs – everything the holidaymaker could want. Best of all were the seaside attractions: the bingo halls and amusement arcades, and stalls that sold candyfloss and sticks of rock. Jason loved rock. He had once taken three hours to suck a stick of aniseed in the hope of finding a fossil inside. Long ago his father had told him that Skegness rock was cut directly from the cliffs by Hunstanton. The lettering, Mr Webberly explained, was an optical illusion made by millions of fossilised plankton. Jason had believed this fable then. Now, of course, he was older and wiser. Now he knew the lettering was etched in the rock by high-powered, infra-red sweetie-lasers – or was that yet another of his dad's tall tales?

He was still thinking about it as the car pulled up beside a large department store called Cloops. Mrs Webberly announced she was popping out a moment to buy some perfume.

"I'll get Hester some *Wild Abandon*," she said.

"I think she's well past *that*," said Mr Webberly.

Mrs Webberly got out of the car. Before she shut the door she made two remarks: one was a curt reply to her husband about people being 'past it', the second was to tell Jason to keep an eye on 'that dog'. As it happened, 'that dog' had been as quiet as a cuddly toy for some minutes. At the first real prospect of open sea he had sprung to his feet, plonked his nose against Kimberley's window and was pawing the glass like a pining pet.

Meanwhile, through the opposite window, Jason was

observing a jolly-looking man in a stripy apron and straw-boater hat. He was trundling an old-fashioned barrow down the sea front and shouting: "Get your cockles here!"

Jason wound his window down. Although he couldn't stand to eat cockles and mussels (they were a bit like swallowing stale chewing gum) he nevertheless adored their vinegary smell.

"Winkles, ninety pence a bag!" yelled the cockle man. The salty seadog pricked his ears. "Fresh from the sea!" the cockle man bellowed. "Juicy, delicious and very..."

"SALTY!" cried a voice. There was a sudden mad scrabble of paws and a brush of fur against Jason's face.

"Daddy! Daddy!" Kimberley squeaked. "The doggie jumped out of the window!"

Mr Webberly gaped in disbelief. "Jason, get out and catch him, quick! Your mum'll have a fit if she knows he's on the loose."

Jason hurriedly unclipped his seat belt.

Mr Webberly scanned the sea front. "Come on, hurry up. He can't have gone far."

"I know where he is!" Kim bounced in her seat.

"Good girl," praised her dad. "Where is he, pebble? Tell Jason which way he ran."

"He hasn't run away," Kimberley said cutely. She pointed through the window. "He just got bigger."

Jason's heart played ping pong against his ribs. There was a pirate right beside the seafood barrow. 'His' pirate. Kimberley must have seen him change.

"Oh yes, that's a pirate," Mr Webberly indulged her. "I expect he's come from a seaside show." He clapped his hands. "Jason! Look sharp. Ask this pirate chap if he saw the dog. Go on, before he moves off."

Jason dived from the car.

By now, a small crowd had gathered round the barrow. The pirate had taken swift advantage of the cockle man's somewhat imprudent offer to sample his products before making a purchase. When Jason skidded to a halt nearby, the pirate was entertaining the crowd by flicking cockles high into the air and catching them neatly on his tongue. Jason was just as impressed as the onlookers and under normal circumstances might have encouraged the show to go on. But when the ornamental clock above Cloops began to chime, his thoughts turned straight away to his mother and the dreadful punishments she was bound to hand out if he didn't get the dog back into the car. So he took a deep breath and shouted to the crowd...

"I'VE LOST MY DOG. HAS ANYBODY SEEN HIM?"

...and prayed the pirate would take the hint.

"I be here, me hearty!" the pirate cried. The crowd began to laugh. Jason grimaced. So much for subtlety. He took a sideways step and tried again. "IF I DON'T FIND HIM QUICKLY MY MUM WILL BE VERY UPSET AND I MIGHT HAVE TO LEAVE SKEGNESS WITHOUT HIM."

With a bump, the pirate arrived at Jason's shoulder. "Be trying these, shipmate!" He offered Jason a haul of winkles. "They be salty 'n' sweaty 'n' rubbery as slugs!"

"Get in the car," Jason hissed.

"What does it look like?" the cockle man asked.

"Blue with a dent on the bumper," blurted Jason.

"Not the car, your *dog*," the cockle man tutted.

"Oh, sorry," Jason said. "He's erm, thin and scruffy and you could easily MISS HIM in a crowd of people. I just wish he'd jump BACK in the car right NOW." He aimed an elbow at the pirate's ribs.

"Stand easy, shipmate," the pirate said, breaking into a vigorous hornpipe. The crowd cheered and clapped their hands. One or two people joined in the dance.

Jason buried his face in his hands. If he didn't come up with something fast, the game would be up and he really would have to leave the dog behind. "Would anyone like to see a trick?" he shouted.

"Aye!" said the seadog. "Can you juggle newts?"

"Shut up," hissed Jason. "You *are* the trick. Do as I say or we're really in trouble." He turned and addressed the crowd again. "I will now turn this pirate into a DOG."

"Go on," scoffed the crowd. "You can't do that."

"I thought you'd lost your dog?" said the cockle man, giving Jason a suspicious look.

"Erm…it's all just part of the show."

"And is all this seafood part of the show? Your mate's had twenty quids' worth, I reckon."

Jason bit his lip. Mum would go spare if she had to fork out twenty pounds for seaside dog food. The pirate was eyeing up the shrimps now, too. Definitely time to make a run for it. "Get ready," he hissed at the dog. He raised his hands and in a loud voice shouted. "ABRA-CA-BLOGGIE, the man becomes a DOGGIE!" Then he twirled round quickly and started for the car. "OK, scarper!"

"Oh no you don't," the cockle man said. He reached out and grabbed Jason firmly by the shoulder. "I had a feeling you pair were trying it on."

"Boo," laughed the crowd. "Rubbish trick."

"It's all *his* fault," Jason said bitterly, trying to give the pirate a kick in the shins. The stupid idiot hadn't changed.

"Twenty quid," the cockle man demanded.

"Squid?" said the pirate. "Be they good 'n' salty?"

"He means money," said Jason. "He wants your…treasure."

"My treasure!" yelled the pirate. "Boggle his britches!"

The crowd of onlookers hollered with delight. "I've a spare doubloon if you're short!" said a voice.

"Give him a broadside!" another advised.

The cockle man was not amused. "Right," he said, and took off his apron. He looked as if he might be handy in a fight. "If you don't settle up, I'll flatten you." The crowd whistled and whooped. Jason panicked.

"But we haven't got any money!" he cried.

"Well, in that case you'd better send Jack Tar here out with a fishing net. One way or another he's replacing those cockles!"

Which turned out to be a rather prophetic statement. At that moment the pirate threw back his head and spat a shower of seafood shells at the cockle man.

"Agh!" he cried. "I've been shot! I've been stabbed!"

A scream went up from one of the women. Suddenly, there was pandemonium in the crowd. An ice-cream fell with a splat to the pavement. The pirate dived forward and lapped it up.

"CHANGE NOW!" Jason begged him "PIRATE, CHANGE NOW!" In the distance, he could see a police car approaching. But a different kind of law was even closer at hand.

"Jason? Is that you?"

"Blistering barnacles," the pirate gulped, "'tis the spawn of the Skegglewitch!" and in the blink of an eye he turned himself into a dog again.

There were one or two awkward questions of course, like, *What were you and that mongrel doing out of the car?* and *Why was that cockle man ranting on about pirates to the police?* Jason just played dumb. He shrugged his shoulders and mumbled incoherently until his mother just frowned and said, "Oh, let's get on."

And on they went, gradually leaving the town in the distance, following a road that was swept by sand and the occasional spray of a crashing tide. Jason had been here many times before, but never had the eeriness pressed in on him so much. His teeth began to chatter as a large old house loomed up in the distance. An old wooden house that seemed to buckle and lean in the midday sun. A house flanked by nothing but shingle on one side and seashore on the other. The car pulled up in an arc of dust. As it settled, Jason looked towards the downstairs windows. They were caked with grime and grit and sand. An old lace curtain twitched. A haggard face appeared at the windows. Two poker-black eyes peered out across the wilderness. Jason swallowed hard and slipped down in his seat.

The eyes belonged to the Skegglewitch, Hester.

Chapter Eleven

"Right," said Mr Webberly, unclipping his seatbelt. "That's my chauffeuring done for now. I'll stop and say hello to the daft old bat, then I'm off to the pub. Fancy a glass of lemonade, Jason?"

"Jason, are you going with your dad or not?" Mrs Webberly glanced over her shoulder. "Jason," she added, a little less evenly, "why has the dog got its head up your sweatshirt?"

Jason looked down at the quaking bump stowing away beneath his clothing. So much for talk of daring deeds. One glimpse of the evil Skegglewitch and the pirate's bravado had fizzled out quicker than a spent firework. "Erm, he saw Aunt Hester and got frightened, Mum."

A dark look clouded Mrs Webberly's face. "Is that meant to be funny, young man?"

"Look out, she's coming," Mr Webberly cut in.

Jason glanced through Kimberley's window. Aunt Hester was hobbling towards the car, leaning heavily against her stick. She was wearing a long, old-fashioned skirt that swept the ground like a lapping tide. Her hair was done up in such a tight perm that it looked as if she'd raided a seashell collection and glued them individually to her head. She peered at the car through her half-moon spectacles. There was a fiery, yet apprehensive glint in her eyes.

Jason wasn't taking any chances. "Quick, abandon ship," he hissed. He poked the seadog once in the ribs and bumped his door open. They tumbled to the ground as if they were practising a parachute roll. Jason heard his mother begin to cluck, but by the time he was on his feet again the dog had scrabbled under the car and Mrs Webberly had gone to intercept the Skegglewitch.

"Hes-terrr," she crooned, giving her a hug and a wide air-kiss. "So lovely to see you again, so soon."

"Speak for yourself," Mr Webberly muttered, pulling a ghoulish face at Jason.

Under normal circumstances, Jason would have laughed. But the churning in his stomach made any sort of grin almost deadly painful. He cast a glance at Great Aunt

Hester. Her hawk eyes darted from face to face. She gave Mr Webberly a long, hard scowl and looked as if she'd like to spit in his eye. Her gaze settled on Jason's mum.

"My dear," she said, like a croaking frog. "Are you well? Is everything quite...*normal?*"

Mrs Webberly affected a laugh. "Of course. What makes you ask?"

Aunt Hester switched her glance to Jason. He tried to back away but a hand with the grip of an eagle's talons almost stopped the flow of blood through his arm. "What about...*the boy?*"

"Oh, quite normal," Mrs Webberly said tiredly. "Acting up all last night, he was."

Aunt Hester pulled Jason close to her face. He flinched as her hooked nose began to twitch. "I can *smell* something about him," she hissed.

Mrs Webberly raised a doubtful eyebrow. "I hope not; he only had a bath last night."

"Something foul and grimy," Aunt Hester continued.

"Probably a drain," Mr Webberly said. Aunt Hester clonked his shin with her stick.

Jason's dad gave a "What did *I* do?" sort of look. Jason had no idea. Glancing down, he saw a grubby paw protruding out from beneath the car. He shifted his weight and kicked it lightly. The paw disappeared without a sound.

"Let's go inside," Mrs Webberly said.

"The bottle," Aunt Hester hissed. "Did you bring my perfume bottle?"

Mrs Webberly patted the bulge in her bag where the gift of *Wild Abandon* lay. "Let's go into the house."

"But did you *bring* it?" Aunt Hester drilled her stick against the ground.

"Hester, calm down," Mrs Webberly soothed. "You don't seem quite yourself today. I'll explain about the bottle, once we're in the house."

"Explain?" Aunt Hester's face turned greyer than a grave-stone. "You mean...?"

"Come along," Mrs Webberly commanded gently. And now it was she with the talon-like grip, turning the frail old woman around. She guided Aunt Hester and Kim indoors.

Jason and his dad both sighed with relief. "Mad old bat," Mr Webberly muttered. He hitched up his trouser leg. A small yellow bruise stood out on his shin. "Did you see that act of unprovoked aggression? We should have set the dog on her. Where *is* the mutt, anyway?"

Jason dropped to his knees and peered under the car. The dog was there with its paws across its eyes. "Come out, you coward!"

"'Tis a terrible prospect," the seadog grizzled.

"All right, stay there. I'll let Dad drive over you!"

The seadog didn't seem to fancy that. With a whoosh it appeared on the far side of the car.

Mr Webberly stared at it over the bonnet. "We really ought to put a lead on Pirate if we're going to take him to the pub, you know."

Jason shook his head. "We're not going, Dad. Me and Pirate, we've got things to do."

The seadog crunkled a lip.

Mr Webberly shrugged. "All right, please yourself. Just don't do anything I wouldn't do."

Jason grimaced. Rescuing a pirate band was hardly part of Dad's normal Saturday afternoon agenda.

Mr Webberly got into the car. "If your mum asks, tell her I've gone to my usual watering hole."

With a *vroom* the car rumbled off.

Jason immediately called Pirate to him. "Come on, we've gotta get moving. As soon as the Skegglewitch learns about your bottle she'll be casting spells quicker than Mum can get a bag on." Quietly, he pushed the front door open. "I'll sneak into the kitchen and steal the key. You stand guard in the hall. If anyone comes, bark your head off."

"Nay," hissed the dog. "If my head be coming off I

might not be getting it on again, boy!"

"Just bark," Jason tutted. "Especially if the Skegglewitch comes."

The old salty seadog flattened an ear. Jason beckoned him to follow and crept into the house. He tiptoed down the long, tiled hall. Paintings of fishing boats and cliff scenes and lighthouses graced every slow and silent step. He glanced back over his shoulder at Pirate. The dog was up on his toes as well. As they sneaked past an ancient maritime barometer, the reading switched from *Fair* to *Inclement*. Jason took a breath and wondered, not for the first time, if he was doing the right thing. But it was a bit too late to change his mind now. He pressed on soundlessly. To his left was the door to the kitchen. Directly opposite that was the lounge. As they drew close, Mrs Webberly's voice came within earshot...

"...well, the bottle wasn't *lost* exactly, but I'm afraid it was...thrown out."

"Thrown out?!" gasped Hester. "But we simply must find it!"

If only you knew, Jason thought darkly. He raised a finger to his lips and ordered Pirate to sit.

In the lounge, Mrs Webberly said, "I got you this as a sort of apology. I'm sure you'll like it. It's been advertised on television." There was a rustle of paper and the clonk of a bottle on a wooden surface.

"My dear, so kind," Aunt Hester said, not sounding in the least bit grateful. "But the bottle? My bottle. Thrown out? Where?"

Jason didn't wait to hear his mother's reply. He dipped into the kitchen and silently opened the pantry door.

Just like the Mother Hubbard nursery rhyme, the pantry was almost bare. There were more cobwebs to eat than pieces of food. But the biscuit barrel was right where he'd predicted: on the top shelf. Jason dragged a three-legged stool across the kitchen, jumped on carefully and reached the tin down. At that moment Aunt Hester's chilling voice boomed:

"BOTTLE BANK?!"

Jason pulled the lid off the barrel, fast. The key was buried among several layers of rather ancient, mouldy digestives. He yanked it out, banged the tin back, then jumped off the stool and hurried to the cellar.

By now, the dog had abandoned his post and was sniffing around the cellar door.

Jason waved him to be quiet and cocked an ear towards the lounge. His mother was still trying to smooth things out.

"I really am dreadfully sorry, Hester. I should have kept a closer eye on Kim."

"The boy," said Aunt Hester, in a voice smeared with deep suspicion. "The boy must know. Where's the *boy?*"

"Walking the doggie," Kimberley said.

A spike of ice touched Jason's spine.

Aunt Hester inhaled like a howling wind; exhaled like a cannon shot. "DOG?!"

The whole house rocked from top to bottom.

Jason didn't hang about. He buried the key first-time in the lock. It turned with a scrape of corroding metal. The cellar door opened with a tired creak. A cool sharp sliver of briny air wafted up a sunken flight of steps.

"Ah," went the seadog, smacking his lips. "Salty 'n' zingy as a sizzled sardine!"

"This is no time to think about food," hissed Jason. "Come on. Let's…get below decks!"

"Aye, aye!" said the dog. With a whoosh he turned himself back into a pirate and clattered down the steps crying, "Cap'n! I be coming!"

Jason said a prayer and followed him in.

The cellar was cold and dank and misty. The only light was the glow from the hall and a weak shaft of sunshine through a slime-covered window. As Jason's feet touched the cobblestoned floor, the soles of his shoes gave a sickly squelch. A dull green mist came swirling about him. It parted with a frantic sweep of his hand, long enough to glimpse what looked like a wine rack clinging in hope to the crumbling walls. He nudged towards it, batting cobwebs and dead flies from his hair.

"Where are you?" he hissed. "Can you see the bottles?"

"Turn up the lamps, boy," the pirate said, his rough voice dying on the streaming walls.

Jason groped around for a switch. His hand brushed against the front of the wine rack and dipped into the murky honeycomb of holes. His fingers closed around a tiny object.

It was a miniature perfume bottle.

"I've found one!" he gasped, flushed with excitement. "It's really, really small. And the stopper's corroded. I think I might be able to pull it out."

"STOP!" cried a voice from the top of the steps.

Jason whipped around. Aunt Hester was silhouetted in the cellar doorway, eclipsing most of the light from the hall.

"Bring that to me," she croaked. "Bring it to me and you will come to no harm." She stretched out a quivering hand.

"N-no way!" spluttered Jason, edging back.

"Give it to ME!" Aunt Hester commanded.

But Jason had already opened his arms. He had the bottle in one hand, the stopper in the other.

There was a tiny whoosh of seaside air.

Grains o' salt! a thin voice squawked.

And out of the bottle came a scrawny parrot.

"It be SWIVEL!" the pirate cried in joy.

Arrk! screeched the parrot, and landed with a whump on Jason's shoulder.

The shock sent Jason stumbling back. He slipped and slithered on the treacherous cobbles. Instinctively, he flung out a hopeful arm and grabbed the nearest thing to hand.

The wine rack.

With a rip of screws from forgiving mortar, it followed him on to the floor.

Bottles tumbled, clattered, smashed.

There was a bellow of anger from the top of the steps.

Jason sat up, rubbing his eyes, and found himself completely surrounded –

by a lot of broken glass...

...and a rather strong smell of stale perfume.

Chapter Twelve

"What on *earth* is going on?"

In a flash, Mrs Webberly appeared in the doorway. The look on her face could have turned a cold rice pudding to gravel. "Jason Webberly, is that you?"

"Yes, Mum," Jason said a bit meekly.

"If you've done what I think you've done, you are in serious trouble, my lad! Get up here, now!"

Jason dragged himself to his feet. There was a grinding crunch of glass underfoot. He blinked in confusion and looked around the cellar. The only pirate he could see was the pirate he knew. And he'd turned into a dog once more.

He also had a parrot sitting on his head.

"What happened? Where are they?" Jason whispered.

"I be confuffled," the seadog whimpered, quaking so

much that the parrot had to flap its wings to stay put. "I be reckoning on shipmates and shanties, boy. Now all I be seeing is the end of a plank."

"JASON, ARE YOU DEAF?! I SAID, GET UP HERE!"

Arrk! went the parrot and loosed a dropping – which just about summed up Jason's mood. No pirates – and now no perfume, either. He was in deep, deep trouble. He trudged up the steps and shuffled shame-faced into the hall. He was met with an instant motherly broadside.

"Oh, look at the STATE of you!"

Even Kimberley, standing in the doorway of the lounge, put a hand to her mouth in shock.

Jason inspected the damage. His trainers were wet with mud and slime and there were bright green stains on both his knees. His upper half hadn't fared much better. His arms were covered in spiders' webs and the front of his sweatshirt reeked of some ancient, rancid scent. *Mummy's Tomb.* That was probably it. Never mind walking a plank, he would probably be thrown in the washer fully clothed.

Before his mother could speak again, Aunt Hester drew Mrs Webberly's fire. "My dear, this is all too much," she simpered. "I fear I'm going to faint." She flopped theatrically against the wall, a limp wrist pressed against her brow.

"Oh, Hester, Hester," Mrs Webberly cooed. She helped the old woman into a chair.

"My perfumes?" said Hester in a quivering voice. "Is there...any hope?"

Mrs Webberly scowled at Jason.

He turned the colour of a Valentine card.

Mrs Webberly grabbed him hard by the ear. "Explain," she snapped, as Kimberley gasped: "Mummy! Mummy! Look, a birdy!"

Jason glanced towards the cellar. The seadog was sneaking round the cellar door with Swivel riding on his head.

Without looking round Mrs Webberly said, "Not now, Kim, go and play in the front room, please."

Kimberley gave a pint-sized huff and stomped off into the lounge.

Jason was made to face Aunt Hester.

"Right," said his mum. "Let's hear it, chapter and verse. You've just ruined a priceless perfume collection. What have you got to say for yourself?"

Jason felt his toes curl inwards. "I was looking for pirates," he mumbled.

Aunt Hester's pale lips twitched.

"PIRATES?" The blast of air from Mrs Webberly's lungs tilted a lighthouse painting askew. "Are you telling me you've been playing some game with that dog?"

"He was in on it," Jason gulped.

Behind a fern-filled vase there came a whining noise. The seadog was padding towards the door, hoping to make a quiet escape. There was little chance of that with a furious Mrs Webberly hot on his tail. "Come here, you disgusting hound!" she bayed.

"Buckets o' bilge!" the seadog whimpered and dived underneath the Welcome mat. Suddenly, Mrs Webberly froze in her tracks. She turned on her heels and glared at the hat stand. There appeared to be a parrot perched on top of it. In a dangerously quiet voice she said, "Where did *that* come from?" She threw Jason an accusing stare.

That was it. Jason could take no more. He could feel a tantrum building inside him and no amount of dark looks was going to quell it. "Ask HER!" he yelled, stabbing a finger at a taut Aunt Hester. "She had it in a bottle. She's an evil WITCH!"

Witch! She be the Skegglewitch! Swivel announced, paddling furiously on the hat stand.

Aunt Hester laid a hand across her chest. "Oh, my dear, the injustice," she croaked. "This is quite the limit."

Mrs Webberly frowned and looked at Swivel. "Hester, is that bird really yours?"

"No, it belongs to the pirates!" cried Jason.

"Be quiet," snapped his mum. "I'm talking to your aunt."

Aunt Hester gave Jason a stare so piercing it felt as if his heart was being burned by a laser. In a low, almost gurgling voice she said, "I bought the parrot for company, my dear, to while away the winter hours. But the bird turned out to have a foul-mouthed beak and I couldn't possibly have it in the house, not when visitors came. So I locked it in the cellar."

"Mum, she's fibbing," Jason whined. "It's three hundred years old. Honest."

Aunt Hester sucked in through her teeth. "My dear, the boy has taken leave of his senses. I demand you throw him out of the house. Might I suggest he be sent immediately into Skegness to find his father and tell him what he's done?"

Mrs Webberly tapped her chin in thought. "Hester, do you know, that's not a bad idea."

"And of course he must take that hideous hound with him."

"So he can do your *task!*" yelled Jason.

Aunt Hester tightened a bony fist.

"Task? What task?" Mrs Webberly demanded. "What nonsense are you on about now?"

Jason gripped his mother's arms. "There's a special gobbet called the saltstone, Mum. She wants it for doing horrible spells. She's sending Pirate on a task to find it."

Mrs Webberly let out an exasperated sigh.

"Mum, it's true! Watch this if you don't believe me." Jason turned towards the dog. "Pirate, show her. Change into a man."

"I be a-feared," the seadog yapped. The Welcome mat shook like a dancing hedgehog. "The witch be making me a lobster's dinner!"

"My dear, send the boy away *now*," growled Hester, slipping a hand towards the pocket of her dress. Jason saw the movement and tensed himself. It was possible the witch was only searching for a tissue, but...

"Pirate, quick! She's up to something!"

Aunt Hester clutched at the lining of her pocket. But whatever she was after didn't seem to be there. Panic flashed across her gnarled old face. Her eyes darted towards the dog. He was sitting up now with the Welcome mat draped over his head.

Mrs Webberly, however, was in no mood for tricks. "Out," she said, spinning Jason round and pointing a finger somewhere into Lincolnshire.

"But Mum, watch Pirate. Then you'll know!"

"Out, the pair of you! I've heard quite enough!"

Arrk! went Swivel.

"You too!" said Mrs Webberly.

Then, just as all seemed lost, Kimberley saved the day. She came at full pelt out of the lounge and skidded to a halt beside her mum: "Mummy! Mummy! Look what I found in Aunt Fester's cupboard!"

Mrs Webberly shifted her focus sideways. "Kimberley, what have I told you about playing with bottles?"

"Bottles?" said Jason, turning to see. From the corner of his eye, he thought he saw Aunt Hester sliding sneakily out of her chair. But for once his concentration was mostly on his sister. Kimberley did have a bottle in her hands. A clear wine bottle.

Inside was an old-fashioned ship.

It was short and squat with a raised poop deck and two masts tilted towards the stern. It had spidery rigging and a proper ship's wheel; an anchor lay rusting on the bottom of the bottle. But the thing that really took Jason's eye was the flag flying from the taller mast. A stout black flag with a white motif. It was the *Jolly Roger,* sometimes known as the skull and crossbones.

The sign of a pirate ship.

Jason bit his lip. His brain began to whirr. Could it

be…? Was it possible that…? He leaned in close and looked for a name. To his surprise the prow of the boat was almost obscured by a thin grey mist, as if the ship was sailing through fog. But several letters were clearly visible, carved on a panel on the upper hull:

The Slippery Skeggle.

Jason gasped out loud. "Pirate, look at—" "this" he was about to say when the words froze in the back of his throat. He gulped and looked again at the ship, hardly able to believe what he was seeing. In the half-barrelled observation post, the crow's nest near the top of the mast, he had spotted a fractional movement. Something had turned and trained a spyglass on him.

It was a tiny pirate.

Chapter Thirteen

"Goodness," Mrs Webberly gasped in surprise, peering over Jason's shoulder. "That's a remarkably lifelike model."

"Mum, it's not a model," Jason panted.

"That be Mr Goggles," an excited voice said.

Mrs Webberly nearly did a backwards flip. A life-sized pirate was standing beside her. "Who in duck's teeth are you?!" she demanded.

"I be Scuttle," he said.

"*Scuttle?*" said Jason. "You mean you've got a name? Why didn't you tell me before?"

"You not be asking," Scuttle said with a shrug.

"Well I'm asking you this," Mrs Webberly growled. "How did you get into this house...you brigand? And what have you done with my aunt?!"

Aunt Hester! Jason whipped around. In all the

excitement of the discovery of *The Skeggle* he'd completely forgotten about Aunt Hester. The chair where she'd been sitting was disturbingly empty.

"The witch be taking her leave," said Scuttle. "She be sneaking tippy-toed to the upper decks when the pipkin be stepping forth with the boat."

"I'll step you forth," Mrs Webberly snarled, slamming her hands into Scuttle's chest and forcing him back down the hall a way. "Get out before I call the police."

"Mum, you already called the police," said Jason. "Scuttle's the dog. We've got to keep him till Tuesday, remember? I told you he could turn into a man. He came out of that bottle I broke. Aunt Hester put a spell on him. Come on, we've gotta run for it before she comes back. I think she's gone to fetch whatever she was looking for in her pocket."

Jason grabbed the bottle and turned towards the door.

Mrs Webberly in turn grabbed him by the collar. "Oh no you don't. You stay *right* here. We're going to wait for Aunt Hester to come downstairs and then we're going to find out exactly what this pantomime is all about."

"But what if she's gone for her spell book or something?"

"Jason, she's probably just gone to the TOILET!"

"Mummy," Kimberley chipped in again, tugging hard at her mother's sleeve.

"Yes, what now?"

Kim pointed at the bottle. Jason and Scuttle peered into it again. By now Mr Goggles was leaning perilously out of the crow's nest, shouting down to the decks below. Though Jason couldn't hear him through the glass, he was pretty sure the pirate was sounding the alarm. Suddenly, another three figures appeared: two through a square-shaped opening in the deck; another from a door at the rear of the ship that Jason took to be the captain's quarters. The solitary figure wore a bright blue jacket, knee-length boots and a three-cornered hat. A thick beard covered most of his face. He pointed a cutlass in Jason's direction and roared an order at the other two men. Jason didn't need to be a lip-reading expert to guess what the order was.

Fire.

Ping! Ping! Ping! Ping! Ping!

From the gunports just below the upper deck a series of mini-lightning bolts splashed and ripped along the length of the bottle.

Kimberley clapped and squealed with delight.

Jason merely squealed and clonked the bottle down on the hall dresser.

"Aar," went Scuttle, shaking a fist. "Mr Candle be seeking to blast a way out! I say we be making wreckings of the bottle!" He lunged forward and grabbed it off the dresser.

"Give me that," Mrs Webberly demanded. She clamped her hands round the neck of the bottle as Scuttle was readying to hurl it to the floor. A furious tussle broke out.

"It be my boat!"

"It belongs to my aunt!"

"I be taking it fair!"

"I be kicking you in the shins if you don't let go!"

The bottle see-sawed this way and that. Pirates cascaded towards the cork, then tumbled into the gently-domed base. Others clung for their lives to the masts and rigging of *The Slippery Skeggle*. Jason grimaced hard. The ship must have crossed some seas in its time, but surely nothing as choppy as this?

Suddenly with a *pop!* the warring parties sprang apart. Scuttle crashed into the empty chair; Mrs Webberly staggered backwards with the cork.

"Drat," she said, staring at the cork as if she'd got a raw deal from a Christmas cracker. She pointed at the bottle. "What's that?" A stream of whitish dust was beginning to whistle up the neck.

"Oh no," Jason trembled as the dust began to puff out and spread into the hall.

Kimberley said, "Is it fiery murks?"

"Sort of," said Jason, shuddering in his socks. He pulled Kim back against the wall.

Whoosh! Whoosh! Whoosh! Whoosh! Whoosh!

A loud A-HAAR! rattled round the hall. A wind that could have filled a dozen sails swirled and bucked from ceiling to floor.

"STAND BY TO BE BOARDED!" cried a frightening voice that sounded like a rake being pulled through gravel.

Mrs Webberly reared back in alarm. "Kimberley, run away and hide," she breathed.

"OK," peeped Kim. She clapped her hands and scooted away. Jason wished his mum had told *him* to run away. If his knees hadn't felt like a couple of sponge cakes he would gladly have legged it, rather than face what had just arrived.

A dizzy-looking band of battle-scarred cut-throats.

The Salt Pirates of Skegness.

Chapter Fourteen

There were six in all – seven including Scuttle. They were the filthiest, ugliest bunch of men that Jason Webberly had ever seen. They looked like a rugby football team that had played ten matches without ever bothering to take a shower. Unlike Scuttle, most of them were dressed in blousy shirts and ragged linen pants sawn off at the knees. Some wore waistcoats or button-up jerkins. Knives and pistols were tucked into their waistbands. Cutlasses hung from their slack leather belts. One thickset pirate with more rings in his ears than could be counted on a curtain pole even had a hook in place of a hand. Jason made a note to steer well clear of him. Yet despite their fearsome, battle-scarred features all the pirates had a sickly ash-grey pallor – a result, Jason thought, of being shaken about. Their eyes were red from the sting of cannon smoke. Most of them were coughing fit to burst.

For a moment, they bumbled around in shocked confusion, trying to get their bearings. Then the bearded pirate in the bright blue jacket, whom Jason took to be Captain Blackhead, quickly asserted command.

"A-haar!" he boomed, jabbing his cutlass high into the air (and almost shaving a feather off Swivel). "I be free and seeking vengeance against the witch! Be plundering, shipmates! We be taking pickings, then making for the shimmering shores to the South. Mr Goggles, what be becoming of the boat?"

THE BOAT!

Jason squealed in alarm. Through the dispersing ruck of bodies he checked the bottle in Scuttle's hand. *The Slippery Skeggle* was starting to dissolve into a dark brown mist. The mist was snaking up the neck of the bottle. Jason fancied he could just make out the creak of ancient shivering timbers. *The Slippery Skeggle* was about to be launched! If it popped out here, the house would be broken to smithereens and anyone near the boat crushed by the hull. Jason took the only course of action possible. Pushing Captain Blackhead aside, he pressed forward and whipped the bottle out of Scuttle's grasp.

With his palm across the opening, he shoved it in front of his shell-shocked mother. "Mum, push the cork in! QUICK!!!"

Mrs Webberly, alert enough to realise the danger, stubbed the cork into the bottle and twisted it down.

At the same moment a cutlass landed *thwap!* on Jason's shoulder. He froze in terror. From close behind his ear Captain Blackhead rasped, "I think Mr Floggem be taking that." Jason gulped as a thin-faced man with silver in his teeth and a cobweb tattoo on his heavily-scarred cheek lifted the bottle out of his hands.

"Right," said Mrs Webberly, pushing up her sleeves. "This has gone far enough."

"Aar," growled the captain, closing one eye. Saliva dribbled into his beard. "I be seeing you bigly through the bottle. You be shaking me overboard. My gizzards be as gribbled as a worm's squidgings. You be paying right dearly for that. Mr Blue Thumb, seize her!"

"No!" cried Jason as a pirate with a hideously swollen thumb clamped a hand across his mother's mouth and dragged her manfully into the lounge.

"What are you doing?" Jason pleaded. "We're on your side. You mustn't hurt Mum. She helped set you free. Ask Scuttle. He knows. He promised there wouldn't be plundering and stuff. He swore on the hairs of a dead man's vest. He said it was shipmates' honour."

"Aar, Mr Scuttle," the captain grizzled. He twisted the cutlass to catch the light, making it wink into Jason's eye. "I be right keen to parley with him. I fancy I be wanting to twist his nose. He be set to guarding *The Skeggle*. I be most anxiously wanting to hear why the boat be snagged in a bottle - and why *Mr Scuttle* not be aboard."

Mr Floggem grabbed a fistful of Jason's sweatshirt. He sneered right into Jason's face. "And I be asking this of you, boy: where be the rest of *The Skeggle*'s crew? There be more legs on a coddling crab than I be counting hands on deck."

"And the prisoner?" Captain Blackhead snarled. "What be becoming of him?"

"Don't know," squeaked Jason. "I don't know about the crew or your prisoner."

Mr Floggem spat on his hand. "Cap'n, be I flogging this scurvy toad?" He whipped a cat-o'-nine-tails out of his belt.

Scurvy toad! carked Swivel, landing on the captain's shoulder.

"Pestersome parrot. Be gone," growled the captain. He gave Swivel a clonk with the hilt of his blade.

Arrk! went Swivel, dropping two feathers. He

fluttered dizzily into the lounge.

The captain scratched his dense, black beard. Two dead maggots and an apple core fell out. "Where be the witch's lair?" he raked. "Speak, boy, or you be for the plank." He flicked the tip of Jason's ear.

"Ow! Don't know."

The captain flicked again.

"I don't know, honest! Mum said she went to the loo."

"Loo?" said Mr Floggem, looking curiously at Blackhead.

"Toilet," said Jason. "The little witch's room."

"The privy?" Mr Floggem chortled darkly. "The witch be about her ablutions?"

The captain slid the ship's bottle into his jacket. "Be seeking her out most carefully, Mr Floggem. Then be reporting directly to me."

Mr Floggem drew a long-barrelled pistol from his belt. "Aye, aye," he sneered, and crept upstairs.

The captain pulled Jason close to his face. Jason did his best not to grimace. Captain Blackhead was not a pretty sight. He looked as if he scrubbed his face with coal then rubbed it twice on a floor mat for luck. There were holes in his hat, stains on his shirt, and blackheads the size of raisins in his nose. He reeked of rum and old damp wood. When he spoke, the barometer casing rattled.

"I be seeking a hardy cabin boy. You be right useful aboard *The Skeggle*."

"I'm not going to sea with you!" spluttered Jason.

"You be doing my orders," the captain growled. "Or I be setting you afloat in a barrel. Away. Be taking pickings!"

With a hefty shove he sent Jason stumbling into the lounge. To Jason's horror, the pirates were running amok. They were climbing the furniture, tearing down the curtains, scoffing Aunt Hester's sandwiches and sponge cake, and filling their pockets with any treasure they could find. Even Scuttle was in on the act. Jason spotted him over by the sideboard stuffing a 'Welcome to Hunstanton' tea cosy into his pocket. He was about to shout something about unkept promises when another pirate picked up a glass decanter, swigged the few millimetres of sherry it contained, then hurled the decanter across the room. It narrowly missed Swivel (who was circling in search of a friendly shoulder) and crashed to pieces in the old-fashioned hearth.

Suddenly a cry of, "Unhand me, you brute!" went up across the room. The irascible Mrs Webberly had dodged her captors and taken a stand in the large bay window. She was locked in a tug-of-war for the phone.

"Give me that," she growled at a ginger-haired pirate with singe marks on his bushy eyebrows. Jason guessed it was Mr Candle, *The Slippery Skeggle*'s master gunner.

"'Tis pickings," said Candle in a squeaky voice. He sounded like a frightened mouse. Jason could imagine him jumping through the deck every time a cannon went off. "I be taking it fair."

"You can take this fair," Mrs Webberly growled and whacked him in the chest with a telephone directory.

Mr Candle crumpled like a lacklustre sail. He toppled over, sending a poker set clattering.

The captain issued a prompt command. "Mr Scabb, that wench be a blight on my eyes, be making her steady, sir."

The pirate with the hook looked up from his looting.

"Mum, look out!" Jason cried, and tried to rush to his mother's aid. Captain Blackhead held him back.

Mrs Webberly, quick to spot her foe, grabbed the first useful weapon to hand: a souvenir hand-bell from Mablethorpe.

"Durr, be surrendering," Mr Scabb demanded. He didn't sound quite the cleverest of pirates, but he was certainly one of the most dangerous-looking. He raised his rusty hook. Jason winced. There were more scars on Mr Scabb's face than you'd see on a cat's scratching post.

The pirate had clearly seen many a skirmish. But it soon became apparent that he had not tackled anything quite as cunning as Shirley Webberly.

"What's that?" she asked. She pointed at Swivel who had landed on a lamp stand.

Mr Scabb turned and scratched his head with his hook (making yet another scar). "Umm, that be the pestersome parrot."

"Quite right," said Mrs Webberly, "and you're about to be as sick as one!" And she clonked Mr Scabb on the head with the bell then kicked him hard in the seat of the pants.

"Suffering seashells," the captain grizzled as his best fighting man was sent sprawling across the dining table to land *splut!* in a piece of sponge cake.

Jason raised a gobsmacked eyebrow. Wow. His mum could *scrap*.

But the odds were not in Mrs Webberly's favour. As she tried to dial the emergency services she was immediately swamped by two more pirates and forced down into a straight-backed chair. A tablecloth was wrapped around her and secured with a braided curtain cord.

"That be right peaceful," the captain said, just as a shout went up across the room.

"Cap'n, there be a pipkin stowed in this hold!"

Mr Blue Thumb was pointing at an open cupboard. Kimberley had tucked herself into the sideboard.

"Jason, do something," his mother fretted.

But Jason was still held fast by the captain.

As it happened, Kimberley didn't seem in the least bit fazed by the mayhem and looting going on around her. She even told the pirate who tugged her out: "You're it, now". She then turned to the sideboard, covered her eyes and started to count.

Suddenly, from upstairs, came a pistol shot. It was followed by an urgent shout: "Cap'n! Cap'n! The witch be stirring!"

The pirates jumped to attention.

Through the crack of the open door Jason saw Mr Floggem coming thundering down the stairs.

"Stand by to skirmish!" the captain roared. He pushed Jason aside and flashed his cutlass.

"Aar!" cried the pirates, rallying to him.

Mr Scabb took an ambush position by the door.

Mr Floggem shouted again: "She be turning to weed and wussely bits!"

Hhh! gasped the pirates, reeling back.

"She be—"

But that was the last Mr Floggem spoke. He had

almost reached the lounge when a bolt of blue lightning flashed down the stairs and *pumff!* he'd disappeared in a wisp of smoke.

In a quivering voice the captain breathed, "Mr Goggles, be reporting, sir."

The ship's look-out peered carefully round the door. "Cap'n, there be nought to goggle."

"Down there," gulped Jason, pointing to the floor.

Mr Goggles refocused his glass. A small green creature with a cobweb tattoo and a cat-o'-nine-tails had just hopped under the nearest chair.

It was Mr Floggem.

Better known now as Mr Froggem.

Chapter Fifteen

Before anyone could even think to say "ribbet", Aunt Hester appeared in the open doorway. She floated in like a dandelion seed, gently blown on a gust of wind.

Mrs Webberly gasped in alarm. "Hester, what are you doing? Hurry away, dear. These men are quite vile."

"These men" didn't look so vile right then. They had backed away into a corner of the bay, gibbering like a bunch of frightened monkeys.

Aunt Hester eyed the pirates through her half-moon specs. "Sooo," she hissed (ignoring Mrs Webberly) "we meet once more, *Captain Blackhead*."

Mrs Webberly tightened her brow in confusion. "Hester, do you *know* these men?"

"'Course she does, Mum! She put them into bottles!"

Aunt Hester whipped around. Jason jumped back and

clonked into the fireplace. There was a powerful knot of fear in his stomach. His aunt didn't look so frail any more. She seemed smug and confident, totally in control. It was just as if when she'd popped upstairs she'd slurped some sort of revitalising tonic that had taken…a hundred years off her. Her pasty-coloured skin was silvery smooth – slimy, almost, like a fish. And her *hair*. It was just as if…

Mrs Webberly was actually the first to comment. "Hester," she said in a calm enquiring tone. "Why are you wearing that dreadful make-up? That seaweed wig does nothing for you. And what is that *awful* smell?"

There seemed to be a stench of rotting trout in the air.

"I am the Skegglewitch," Hester breathed, in a voice that sounded like bubbles being sucked up through a straw. "You will be silent and obey my commands."

Mrs Webberly scowled rather darkly at that. Had she been able to push up her sleeves she very likely would have done. "I think you'd better untie me," she said. "And explain precisely what is going on."

"Very well, *my dear*." Aunt Hester threw out a hand. The tablecloth binding Mrs Webberly to the chair unwrapped itself and sailed across the room (almost blanketing most of the pirates, who flapped in alarm and tossed it aside).

Mrs Webberly stood up and dusted herself down. "Thank you. Now, let's have one thing clear. Any more unpleasant remarks and I will take the children and go straight home."

Aunt Hester rattled with annoyance. "Fool. You will never leave Shingle Towers." She pointed a wussely finger and rapped:

> You will polish, dust and shine,
> My maid you'll be till the end of time.

With a *pop!* an apron appeared round Mrs Webberly's waist; a feather duster in her hand. She blinked twice as the spell began to register, then surveyed the lounge with a critical eye. "Tch, what a terrible mess," she tutted. "I suppose you brigands are to blame for this?"

"Aar," growled the brigands, looking rather guilty.

"Mum, run away!" Jason begged.

"Run away?" Mrs Webberly queried. "With all this tidying up to be done? I hardly think so, Jason. Dustpan and brush. That's the order of the day." With a sigh she poddled off to find them.

Aunt Hester turned to the cowering pirates. "The boat," she growled. "Hand it to me."

"We never be surrendering *The Skeggle!*" roared Blackhead. He bravely sported his cutlass.

Aunt Hester turned it into a windmill. With another wave of her hands the pirates' knives became lollipop sticks and their pistols ended up as harmless carrots (Mr Scabb took a bite of his). Mr Floggem, still hopping about on the floor, had his cat-o'-nine-tails turned into a mop.

The captain, grinding what teeth he possessed, hurled his trusty windmill aside. "Stand fast and be fighting fair!"

"Stand fast," mused Hester. "What a splendid idea." Without another word she put back her head and spat out a putrid purple substance, best described as *wussely goo*. It splattered around the pirates' feet and set like week-old chewing gum. They were immediately held fast where they stood.

"Now," growled the Skegglewitch, beginning to advance. "Hand me the boat or—"

"Coming, ready or not," said a voice.

It was Kimberley. She was still facing the sideboard, counting, completely oblivious to the drama around her.

"What is this foolish child doing?" spat Hester.

"She's only playing hide-and-seek," gabbled Jason. "Don't hurt her. Let her go."

Kim jumped round, pulling up her socks. "You smell," she said, pinching her nose. She made an ugly face at her aunt.

Aunt Hester prodded Kimberley's shoulder. "Go away

you meddlesome fly, or I will dangle you from the washing line and use you up as sparrow food."

Kimberley stuck out her tongue.

Aunt Hester did not take this well.

> Wind and rain and salt of Skeggle,
> Turn this pipkin to a pebble.

A miniature thunderstorm exploded over Kimberley's head. In its wake a small grey pebble clattered to the floor.

That was it for Jason. "You turn my sister back!" he cried and came stomping forward with his fists raised high.

In a flash more goo shot out of the Skegglewitch's mouth. Jason found himself quickly cocooned in what looked like seaside candyfloss. He struggled in vain but couldn't move.

Aunt Hester clicked her fingers. The pebble jumped neatly into her pocket. She flashed her gaze at the helpless pirates. "Now, where is the BOAT?"

"It be hid!" the captain tried to bluff.

"Then we shall *sniff it out*," said the witch. Another spell left her fishy lips:

> Snivelling seadog, filthy wretch,
> Skeggling bottle you will FETCH!

At the back of the pirate group, Scuttle changed silently into a dog. His shipmates, still gummed tight to the floor, failed to see the transformation. Jason kept his silence and watched. The seadog, paws unglooped from the goo, padded forward, nose to the ground. There was a strange, almost trance-like look in his eyes. His pupils had turned completely white.

"What be this?" said Mr Blue Thumb as the dog came snuffling around his knees.

Mr Goggles trained his spyglass on Scuttle. "This cur be remarkable familiar. I be goggling it afore, but I not be knowing where."

"Durr, it be having a kerchief," said Mr Scabb.

"And a patch," squeaked Mr Candle. "And cloggy paws."

"It be right piratey," the pirates agreed.

"'Tis an ugly fudkin," Mr Blue Thumb muttered.

Ugly fudkin! Swivel carked.

Aunt Hester lobbed a banana at the bird and spat a curt command at Scuttle: "Mark the one with the boat. Hurry."

The seadog paused by the captain's feet. He sniffed the captain's jacket pockets. "It be you," he yapped and cocked a leg. He piddled freely on the captain's boots.

"Snivelling starfish!" the captain cried. "I be tying

you to *The Skeggle's* anchor and dragging you along the seabed, you cur!"

Aunt Hester cackled and spiralled a finger. The bottle whizzed out of the captain's pocket and winged its way to her wrinkled hands. "Ah, such a fine old ship," she said. "What a pity to have to turn it to *driftwood.*"

"Nay!" cried Blackhead. "Spare the boat!"

There was anger and despair in the captain's voice. For the first time, Jason felt sorry for the pirates. That ship was their home. It was everything to them. Their spirit would be broken if *The Slippery Skeggle* was turned to splinters.

A smug grin lit up the witch's face. "Captain, calm yourself," she purred. "We had a deal once; we could have another."

"I not be quaffling your potions," he growled.

"You know what I want," Aunt Hester snapped. "Bring me the stone and the ship is yours. You are then free to sail away."

Jason said, "But I thought Scuttle was bringing you the—?"

"Silence, you wart," the Skegglewitch hissed. "Captain, what is your answer?"

The captain growled and scratched his beard. Two dice and an ace of spades fell out. "The stone be aboard

The Skeggle," he grizzled.

The Skegglewitch tightened her hands round the bottle. "It is not," she hissed, looking rather peeved. "Three hundred years ago, Mr Scuttle fired it out to sea..."

"Treachery!" yelled the pirates.

"It was an accident!" cried Jason. "He didn't mean to do it!"

"Be still!" Aunt Hester growled. "Or I shall turn your tongue to a jellyfish."

Jason pressed his lips together. Aunt Hester turned to the pirates once more. "The stone has been found. It lies in a tavern at the centre of the town, at the sign of The Dancing Fish."

Dancing Fish! carked Swivel.

The Skegglewitch gurgled with fishy impatience and crossed one finger over another.

Hrrk! went Swivel as his beak did the same. *Duncing Fosh*, he reported tamely.

The captain called the crew into a huddle. After much gruffling, he turned to the Skegglewitch again and asked, "How be we finding this dancing fish?"

"Mr Scuttle has a map beneath his kerchief."

The captain's face turned blacker than his boots. "Mr Scuttle? He be party to some hornswoggling business of late. How be a deckhand be coming by a map? He be less use than a leaking bucket!"

"Why not ask him?" the Skegglewitch said. She rolled her fingers and the glazed look passed from the seadog's eyes. Aunt Hester made an upward movement with her hand. With a whimper, the seadog grew into a man.

"Spit, gob and fishbones!" the captain growled. "You be widdling on my boots!"

"Cap'n, I be ordered by the witch!" Scuttle trembled.

The captain ignored this pitiful plea. With a swipe of his grimy hand he whipped Scuttle's kerchief off his head. He unfolded the map and studied it well. "There do be a cross at the sign of a boat."

"That be a treasure map for sure," the crew murmured.

"Then we have a bargain?" the Skegglewitch hissed.

"Aar," went the pirates. "Be setting us free."

The Skegglewitch flapped a hand. The goo disappeared from the pirates' feet. Mr Floggem reappeared and Swivel found he could cark again. "You have until high tide this evening," rapped Hester. "Fail and the boat will be splinters and dust."

"To the tavern!" cried the captain, waving the map.

"A-haar!" cried the crew. "Cap'n, what be we doing with Scuttle?"

"Be we winkling his nose hairs?!"

"Be we burning his kerchief?"

"Be we filling his clogs with the gizzards of a gull?"

"Be we turning his eye patch *the other way out?*"

The captain raised a hand. "Mr Scabb, pay heed. Mr Scuttle be under your guard. He be on a *charge*."

"The plank for Scuttle!" the pirates roared. And with a thunder of clogs they exited the house.

Aunt Hester rubbed her hands with satisfaction. "Well, a splendid afternoon's work," she said. "The pirates on a mission they dare not fail, your annoying mother turned into my housemaid, your irritating sister reduced to a pebble."

"W-what about me?" Jason stammered.

"Ah yes, *you*," the Skegglewitch said.

And gave him an evil smile.

Chapter Sixteen

With a twizzle of her fingers Aunt Hester swept away. Before Jason could even think to squeak "Help!" he found himself drawn into a spiralling vortex like an egg being whisked into a pudding bowl. His body zipped through the air, stretching and twisting like a piece of elastic. It felt as if his skin was being dragged off his bones. The journey only lasted a gut-churning second, though it felt like the longest roller-coaster ride in history. It ended with a painful, squelching *splat!*

Back in the cold damp cellar.

"W-what are we doing here?" he gulped. The goo had disappeared from his body now. He was sitting on the floor among the broken bottles. Aunt Hester was standing directly in front of him, tapping her evil fingertips together. She didn't answer the question straight away.

"I suppose you thought you were being clever, interfering with my plans? You must have been quite disappointed, boy, to find no pirates imprisoned here? That was my little ruse, I'm afraid. I *moved* them when I knew that Scuttle was missing. I suspected he would try a rescue mission."

"You're horrible," said Jason, getting to his feet. He pulled his damp trousers away from his bottom. "You shouldn't have made Scuttle wee on the captain. They'll make him walk the plank."

"It is all he deserves; he failed his task."

"He never had a chance!" Jason said hotly. "He got blown off course – to Leicester."

"Ah yes," Aunt Hester rasped, a glob of saliva fizzing from her teeth. "That was all thanks to your dunce of a father. I will turn him to frog spawn when I see him next."

"You leave Dad alone. What's *he* done?"

"Everything!" Aunt Hester spat. "Last Saturday afternoon, I dropped Scuttle's bottle in your father's jacket. He should have carried it straight to the tavern. For some reason, which only your father knows, the bottle did not reach its destination. If it had, the stopper would have popped from the neck and the idiot dog would have sniffed out the stone. It was a brilliant plan. It should not have FAILED!"

"Tough, it *did!*" Jason wanted to shout, but he wisely bit his tongue. In his present predicament, it might not be sensible to irritate the witch. What's more, the longer he could keep her talking the more chance he had of thinking up a means of escape. He had seen this lots of times in films. If the hero (him) asked the baddie (her) questions, the baddie might slip up and give something away. Something the hero might use to his advantage. So Jason spluttered out, "W-what tavern?"

Aunt Hester grizzled with impatience. "*The Dancing Fish*, you whelk. The public house where your father takes his ale."

Jason frowned and pictured Scuttle's map in his mind. So that was what the drawing of the fish was about. It was a mark to show Scuttle where the stone was located: in a pub called The Dancing Fish. But on the map, the cross was drawn on a boat. So Jason posed the logical question: "Does the tavern look like a ship?"

"Yes," said the witch, grinding her teeth.

"Why's the stone there? Who found it?"

"That is not important," Aunt Hester said grittily. "All that matters is that *I HAVE IT!*"

She spat these last few words so fiercely that Jason winced and covered his face. He was waiting for his short life to flash before his eyes when, surprisingly,

Aunt Hester tottered. "The stone," she muttered, wheezing deeply, "too many spells...power diminishing...must replenish." Her hand fumbled in the pocket of her skirt. This time she found what she was looking for: a small yellow box, decorated with drawings of seaweed and shells. She flipped the box open. A sparkling blue light winked around the cellar. It was coming from a fragment of crystalline stone.

Saltstone, Jason thought.

So that was why Aunt Hester had gone upstairs: to fetch her piece of the *stone*. She obviously needed it to boost her powers. To top up her batteries, so to speak. Without it, she was nothing but a frail old stick.

With a mixture of fascination and awe, Jason watched Aunt Hester break the fragment of stone in two. She placed one of the flecks back into the box and the other on the tip of her lizard-like tongue. She took it quickly into her throat. At once, her body shuddered and quaked. From her lungs came an awful gurgling sound like water finding its way down a plughole. For one terrifying second her skin seemed to turn completely transparent and Jason saw – not the skeleton of a human – but something very fishy indeed. Something made of tentacles and scales and fins.

The true Skegglewitch.

"You're a monster," he said, breathing hard.

"Too kind," said the witch, refreshed once more. "But you haven't seen anything *yet*."

Jason's palms went clammy with fright. "Oh yeah?" he taunted as casually as he could. If he remembered correctly, this was the bit in the film where the evil baddie boasted of her plans while the hero looked around for the means to do her in.

"When the whole of the stone is mine," cackled Hester, "I will possess sufficient power to make my transformation complete." With that, she sang a little rhyme:

I shall be eternal. Queen of the Sea.
A mermaid like no other I'll be!

"A mermaid?!" Shocked by this new revelation, Jason put his escape plans on hold. "You can't be a mermaid. Mermaids are nice."

"They're due for a change of *image*," snarled the witch. "Horrible, cutesy, hair-brushing creatures. When I rule the seas and can breathe underwater, all mermaids will become my willing servants. If they resist, they're for it, hah! (She drew a line across her neck and clicked her tongue). Same goes for whales."

"What's wrong with whales?" Jason was feeling very hurt now. He rather liked whales.

"Useless, blubbery things," said the witch. "Take up far too much space in the sea. And as for those frothy little seahorses…I shall snack on them until I burst. They're very over-rated."

"You're mad," said Jason.

"Naturally," said the witch. "I am also tired of your snivelling prattle." She flapped an angry hand. With a turbulent clinkle the broken glass around the cellar floor gathered itself into bottles again. "Now, which one shall be yours?" She studied the bottles like a child at play. "If you're going to be shrunk for ever and a day we want you to be as *uncomfortable* as possible. The red one, I think." She pointed at a squat red bottle that didn't look deep enough to hold a drop of ink.

"I'm not going in there!" squeaked Jason. Now, of course, was the moment in the film when the hero created the great diversion and scooted up the steps to rescue his family and save the world from the evil menace. But all Jason could do was back away tamely. He was stopped by a cold, wet wall. He put out his hands and grasped at the stones. Maybe he'd find a weapon there? He didn't. He found a nest of woodlice. They woke from their huddle and scrambled irritably over his fingers. Jason squealed and batted them off. He hurled the last at Great Aunt Hester.

She ate it, and burped.

"And another thing," she hissed. "When I have the stone I shall put a spell on woodlice to make them less gassy."

"Well if *I* ever get the stone," cried Jason. "I'll make sure you get turned to…GUBBINS!" (It was the best thing he could think of on the spur of the moment.)

Aunt Hester cackled so loudly the bottles jiggled on the cobble-stoned floor. "You?" she jeered. "What could *you* do with the stone? You may be of my skeggling blood, but no *boy* has ever worked the saltstone's power. The stone has strange effects on *boys*. Why, your little sprat of a sister would pose a far greater threat than—" Suddenly, Aunt Hester jerked back her head. Her evil eyes narrowed. She had the look of a witch who'd said too much. "Enough," she snapped, "it's time for your bottle." She lifted her hands to cast the spell.

"Wait!" cried Jason. "I want to ask you something."

"If you need the toilet, wee in the bottle!"

"I don't need the toilet. I just want to know why you're being so horrible to us – turning Kim to a pebble and Mum to a maid? We've never done anything horrid to you."

"Hmm, tricky one," Hester mused. "You *are* part of my family, I suppose. Oh yes, that's it. You're part of my family. I have to be rid of you so that when I become the Queen of the Seas none of you can ever challenge my throne. Right, think tiny thoughts."

"Wait!" squeaked Jason, flapping his arms in desperation. "I'll... I'll..."

"Hurry up," growled Hester. "You'll... you'll... what?"

"I'll make you a deal!"

"Deal?" The Skegglewitch cocked an evil ear.

Jason nodded. At last an idea had perched in his brain. "Let *me* get the saltstone for you."

Aunt Hester's eyebrows twitched.

"I can make it into town much quicker than the pirates. I could…catch the bus! I can get a return ticket! I'll find Dad, in the pub. He'll help, he's bound to – once he knows you've got Mum and Kimberley. That's the deal, OK? I bring you the stone; you turn Mum and Kimberley back."

Aunt Hester picked at the mole on her chin. "Not good enough," she snapped. "Your stupid father will foul things up. Besides, the pirates dare not fail. Prepare to be shrunk."

Jason panted with fright. Now there was only one thing for it: he had to start lying through his teeth. "But…the pirates are going to do the dirty on you!"

The Skegglewitch hissed and wiggled her nose.

"Double-cross *me*? They would not dare."

"It's true! I heard the captain telling Mr Floggem that when they'd got the stone they'd keep it and forget about *The Slippery Skeggle*. Then they'd go off and find another boat. And there was nothing you could do cos you'll DIE without the stone – I hope – I mean – you will, *won't you...*?"

The Skegglewitch shook with rage. "I will shrink them and dip them in lobster jam then clamp them in oysters and bake them in the sun!"

Jason winced. Ugh, pirate waffles. Very nice, not.

"Very well," the Skegglewitch seethed, leaning so close that Jason could see himself reflected in her specs. "You would be a waste of a good bottle anyway. It is true that I will wither if I do not have the stone. But if *I* go so does your father's precious pebble." She grinned and took 'Kimberley' out of her pocket. "You have until high tide this evening. If the stone is not in my hands by then I will cast this pebble on to the beach where there are millions of others like it. You will never find your irksome sister again, especially after the *sea* rolls in."

"You're evil!"

The Skegglewitch shook her skirts and sighed. "Of course I'm evil. It's my job. Well? What are you waiting for? The buses are every twenty minutes on a Saturday."

Jason bit his lip. There *was* one problem. He had now, in effect, set himself in competition against the pirates. What if they succeeded and he failed? Would Aunt Hester still set Kimberley free?

"No," she said with a fishy sneer. "If Blackhead returns the stone, your sister remains a piece of shingle; if *you* arrive first, their boat turns to splinters."

"But...that's not fair!"

"Fair?!" the Skegglewitch blasted. "Fair is a word for pathetic little earwigs."

"What about Scuttle?"

The Skegglewitch cackled. "Scuttle is doomed, both ways. If the pirates get their boat, he walks a plank; if you beat them to it, he stays a mutt for the rest of his days. Quite entertaining, isn't it?"

"We're shipmates," said Jason. "I want to save him."

"How touching," Aunt Hester muttered, sucking a dead fly off her arm. "Very well, I will make you one concession. The dog may yet be of use. If you guide him to the tavern he will sniff out the stone. If he returns with you, I will lift his curse."

"But the pirates have got him."

"Then you must use your wits to free him. Now hoppit, you whelk – and *no tricks*."

Jason bounded up the cellar steps. "You don't scare me," he shouted defiantly.

Aunt Hester roared with anger and turned her face into a shark's head.

"All right, you do scare me!" squeaked Jason. And he scooted out of the house.

Chapter Seventeen

As he hurried up the drive towards the old sea road, Jason found himself thinking hard about Kimberley. Why had Aunt Hester stopped so abruptly when she'd been talking about his sister? What did she mean, Kim might be a threat? Kim was a child. A little girl of five. Even if she did get hold of the stone, how could *she* be a threat to a Skegglewitch?

Whatever the answer to that question might be, it was driven out of Jason's mind right then by a clatter of clogs and a blast of *A-haar!* Until that moment, the only thing moving on the old sea road had been tufts of marsh grass wafting in the wind. Now, from behind a clump of bushes, came the Salt Pirates of Skegness.

"Where be you roving?" the captain growled, immediately reeling Jason in. "Mr Goggles be spying you leaving the Towers. We be hiding ourselves most tidily in the shrubbery while we be watching your sneaky jaunt. Mr Floggem be right eager to know how you be escaping the witch?"

Mr Floggem spread his mop across Jason's shoulder.

"She threw me out," Jason answered boldly. There was no point being weedy now. If he was going to accomplish his task, he had to row in with the pirates for a while. "She said I wasn't worth bottling. So I've come to infiltrate – I mean, join your crew. I'd like to be a fearsome seadog, please."

Aar, went the pirates, raising their fists. Mr Scabb, who'd been holding Scuttle by the ankles and shaking him to see if any more treasure maps might be hidden about his person, let his captive crumple to the ground.

Captain Blackhead scratched his beard in thought. A few mouse droppings and a mushroom fell out. He exchanged a brief word with Mr Floggem, then beckoned Jason close. "I be giving you a piratey test. To be a seadog true, you must be goggling over this chart and reckoning on its meaning, aar."

He flashed the map at his shipmates.

Aar, the pirates echoed quietly, chortling into their grimy palms.

"Suffering seashells," Jason said cleverly. "That's a hard test."

It wasn't, of course. He knew exactly what the pirates were up to. They hadn't got a clue how to read the map. They needed him to tell them where to go. For one wonderfully wicked moment he was tempted to send them up the coast to Cleethorpes, but if he did they would only take him with them and that would mean no one would get the stone. So he quickly went through the map, 'guessing' at what the landmarks might be. He even worked out what the pawprints were for. If Dad had been successful and delivered the bottle, the doggy tracks were there to show Mr Scuttle the quickest route *back* to Shingle Towers: straight up the beach.

"*Aar*," went the captain, looking pleased with himself at the wealth of information he'd 'prised' from the boy. "That be our homeward bearing, shipmates. We be clogging the sand once the stone be ours."

The pirates roared once more.

Meanwhile, Jason was plotting almost as fast as his brain could whirr. "Trouble is, the map will help you find the tavern, but the stone is hidden in a secret place. Only a dog can sniff it out."

"Mr Scuttle be a mangy cur!" cried the pirates. "We be following his doggy snout!"

Jason glanced at the ill-fated pirate. Mr Scabb had his hook on Scuttle's shoulder. It was going to take something extra special to prise the old seadog out of this mess. So Jason went for the biggest fib of the lot: "You'll never get the stone if you make him walk the plank and he only changes to a dog if you know the proper spell."

An unsettled murmur rumbled round the crew. Scuttle himself looked a little perplexed.

"Be showing us this spell," Captain Blackhead hissed.

Mr Scabb thrust Scuttle forward. Jason whispered in Scuttle's ear, "Change when I tell you. It's your only chance. But *don't* do it for anyone else, OK?" He stood away quickly and waved his arms in a wizardly manner. "Abracabloggie, the man becomes a doggie!"

With a miserable whine, Scuttle turned into a dog.

"Aar," went the pirates, biting their knuckles.

"Now turn back," Jason whispered. He clicked his fingers and gave the dog a kick. Scuttle turned back into a man.

Captain Blackhead scratched his beard. Two buttons and a rusted nail fell out. "Be saying the spell more slowly, boy. I not be catching it right."

Abracabloggie, the man becomes a doggie! Swivel carked from the flag of a bus stop.

138

"A-haar!" cried the captain. "The parrot be having it!" With a swirl of his arms he boomed the spell.

"Won't work," said Jason (mouthing a quick *don't change* at Scuttle). "It's not *what* you say it's *how* you say it." He paused to breathe on his nails. "I suppose that I've just got the knack. Carry on like that and you'll be turning people into frogs, not dogs."

Mr Floggem, who had no wish to be a frog again, made a hasty suggestion. "Cap'n, I say we desist with witchery and be urgently finding the fishy tavern."

"Aar," went several members of the crew.

The captain wiped a piece of snot off his nose and quickly called a meeting of his senior men. After much whispering and a few restrained *aars*, he turned to Mr Scabb. "Mr Scabb," he said in a voice more slippery than a fish dock at Grimsby, "be unhooking Mr Scuttle if you please. I reckon I be doing him pitifully poor. It be grave misfortune to be toggled with a cur. Mr Scuttle be a trustful member of the crew. He be sniffing out the stone most gladly, I reckon. B'aint that be so, Mr Scuttle?"

"I be serving most proudly!" Scuttle beamed, relieved to be back in the captain's favour.

"And you, boy," Captain Blackhead continued, throwing an arm round Jason's shoulder. "You be most eager to assist Mr Scuttle? You be saying the spell when the stone be nigh?"

Jason took a glance at Mr Floggem. The tattooed pirate was grinning slyly at Mr Blue Thumb, who in turn was winking at Mr Goggles. Jason knew they weren't to be trusted. But that didn't matter – neither was he.

"Aye, aye – Cap'n."

"Aar!" The captain spat on his hand and thumped his new shipmate heartily in the back. "Then you be a Skeggler true. To the stone, shipmates. Come, boy, you be knowing these parts. How best be we roving to the sign of the fish?"

"Cap'n, we be boarding a chariot," said Scuttle, already buzzing with his new found importance. "'Tis uncommon swift passage. I be roaming in one!"

"And I be a nine-legged newt," said the captain, just as a car came speeding round a bend. It nearly swerved into the nearest marsh at the sight of a bunch of moth-eaten pirates legging their way along the verge.

"That be a chariot," Scuttle beamed as the pirates (bar him) all dived for cover. Swivel joined a gull on top of a lamp post from where he loosed a dropping on the captain's hat. It was the brightest moment in Jason's afternoon.

"Scuttle's right," he said. "You have to wait here – for

a really big chariot." He planted himself by a wonky bus stop.

The pirates crept across the road to join him. Mr Blue Thumb eyed the pole with interest. "Be we uprooting this short mast, boy, and running the chariot through before boarding?"

Jason shook his head. "You just put out a hand and the chariot stops."

The pirates muttered amongst themselves. "'Tis a witching pole, then? Be there a special incantation?"

"Sort of," Jason replied. "You say: "One to The Dancing Fish" and the chariot takes you there."

"I be spying one, Cap'n!" Mr Goggles reported. He pointed down the road.

Sure enough, a single-decker bus had just eased round the bend. All the pirates put out a hand. The chariot rumbled to a stop. The confused-looking driver, a man in his fifties, leaned forward in his cab and peered through the windscreen.

"One to The Dancing Fish!" roared the pirates.

"Not until he's opened the doors," Jason tutted.

The doors wheezed open.

"Right then, what's all this?" asked the driver.

"We be going to the tavern!" the captain boomed.

The driver didn't seem at all surprised. "Aye, you look

141

like you've downed a few pints in your time."

Jason stepped on to the bus. "One child, seven pirates and a parrot, please."

"No parrots," said the driver. "Are they with you? Blackbeard's mob? Or is the panto running late this year?"

"His name's Black*head*, and they're real. Can the parrot ride on the wing mirror?"

The driver puffed his cheeks. "It's a bit irregular. I'm not licensed to transport livestock – or pirates." He scoured the motley crew. "Are they, y'know, properly *laundered*? They smell a bit socky if you get my drift. They're making me itch just looking at them. We might never get the stains off the seats."

"Please, just take us into town," begged Jason.

The driver sighed and checked his fares. "All right. Sixty pence for you; one-twenty each for Jack and his Tars; the parrot can travel as a minor."

Jason patted his pockets for money. All he possessed was a conker and half an elastic band. He turned to the pirates. "We can't go, unless we give him treasure."

"Boggle his britches!" the pirates cried.

Mr Scabb leapt on to the bus. "Huh-hurr! Stand by to be boarded!" he hollered.

The bus driver wasn't having any of that. Quick as a

flash he leapt to his feet and struck Mr Scabb with a bag of spare change.

Mr Scabb tumbled backwards down the step, knocking over most of his shipmates in the process.

The bus driver wagged a warning finger. "Pay the right fare or you're off," he growled. He pulled his cuffs from the sleeves of his jacket.

Jason turned to the pirates again. "We've got to do a trade. It's...the custom."

The pirates muttered grievously and emptied their pockets. Amongst the cutlery and ornaments and pieces of cake, Jason spotted a carriage clock. He whipped it out of Mr Candle's swag and offered it up to the bemused driver. "Will this do – for all of us?"

The driver coughed into his fist. "Does it work?"

Jason held it out. The carriage clock ticked.

"Done," said the driver. "But I'm short on change."

"Keep it," said Jason and plonked himself down in the nearest seat.

"A-haar!" cried the pirates and stormed up the steps. They charged to the back of the bus and started to haggle over who should sit where.

Anchors aweigh! carked Swivel, clinging tight to the wing mirror.

"Settle down, please," the driver called.

Jason wished he could settle his nerves. In less than ten minutes the bus would arrive in the centre of Skegness. Then the search for the stone would begin.

Chapter Eighteen

As the bus sped away, Jason beckoned Scuttle to join him. The pirate came lamping down the aisle and plonked himself on the seat beside the boy. "This be a fine adventure," he beamed.

"Hardly," sighed Jason. "We need to talk." He glanced over his shoulder. Fortunately, no one was watching them. Mr Goggles was spying out the coastal horizon. Mr Scabb and Mr Blue Thumb were standing on the seats, having a mock sword fight with a couple of rolled-up magazines. The captain appeared to be taking bets on which of them would get an ear cuffed first.

"When we reach the town," Jason whispered. "You and me have got to run away."

Scuttle gazed across the broad grey waters to their right.

"Not to sea," Jason tutted. "We've got to find the

saltstone and take it to the house."

Scuttle cocked his head proudly. "Aye, I be sniffing it out for the captain. I be much in his favour, boy."

Jason shook his head. "He's stringing you a line."

Scuttle tugged his earring and looked a little puzzled. "We be running away to fish for spratlets?"

Jason slapped a hand across his brow. "*No-oo*, he's using you. He just wants you to *think* you're in his favour so you'll sniff out the stone when he's ready. Once he's got it and he wins back the ship, he's still going to make you walk the plank. *And* he's going to take me to sea. I'll be swabbing decks for the rest of my days."

Scuttle gave a quiet shrug. "'Tis a worthy profession with a decent bucket."

Jason whopped him hard in the thigh. "It'll serve you right if you end up as crab food. I'm trying to save you. None of this was supposed to happen. You promised there wouldn't be plundering and stuff."

The old salty seadog tilted his head. "'Twas but a few trinkets," he said (examining a handy set of coasters he'd filched).

"I'm not talking about *trinkets*," Jason argued. "I'm talking about my mum and sister. If I don't beat Captain Blackhead to the stone, Mum'll stay a maid, Kim will be a pebble and *you'll* be eating biscuits for the rest of your life."

"I be right partial to a tasty biscuit."

"*Dog* – biscuits," Jason pointed out.

Scuttle winced at that.

Just then the bus lurched to a halt. Two noisy youths jumped on. They slung a few coins at the driver and came down the bus with a pompous swagger. They were dressed in T-shirts, jeans and trainers. Each of them was carrying a packet of crisps.

"Oh no," thought Jason, reading the flavours: 'Ready Salted' and 'Salt and Vinegar'.

"What be this?" snarled the captain, eyeing the pair.

"Nice hat, Grandad," one of them snickered. They bounced into a seat and opened their crisps.

Jason covered his eyes.

From the wing mirror came a familiar cry: *Grains o' salt!*

"SALT?!!" cried the pirates.

The crew leapt to their feet. One youth had a crisp as far as his lip when, to a man, the salt pirates swooped.

"What's going on there?" the bus driver asked, peering into his rear-view mirror.

"Those lads are just sharing out their crisps," said Jason.

The captain stood back wiping his mouth. "Aar, they be right tasty!" he declared, and let out a hideous burp. "Where be we finding more vittles like these?"

The youths just sat there, open-mouthed.

With his usual sneer Mr Floggem asked, "Cap'n, be we pressing these maggots for crew? They be useful for scraping the belly of a cannon."

"And skinning whelks," Mr Blue Thumb added.

Both youths pinged the bell. "Wewannagetoff!" they gabbled at the driver.

"Make your mind up," he tutted. "You've only just got on!"

"Don't care! We'll walk to town!"

The driver grumbled and pulled into a stop.

The youths fled.

There were no more passengers after that. But it wasn't the end of the drama on the bus. Another half mile along the road, a cry went up from Mr Goggles: "Wreck ahoy!"

"A-haar!" cried the pirates, and pressed themselves almost flat to the windows.

Jason peered out of his. All he could see was a field full of caravans and the first few signs of seaside guest houses. The bus was nearing town.

The captain ordered Mr Goggles to report.

Mr Goggles adjusted his glass. "It be a pirate boat, Cap'n. It be flying the bones."

"Be it headed this way?"

Mr Goggles shook his head. "It be shot through and listing."

"Be there treasure spilled?"

"Aye, Cap'n. There be barrels and chests."

"Pickings!" roared the pirates, slapping palms.

"What's he on about?" Jason asked Scuttle. They switched to the other side of the bus. From this view, if he squinted, Jason could just make out the clock tower at the centre of the sea front and the promenade which led straight down to the beach. He cast his eye farther, out across the sea. The sun was low in a clouded sky, its long rays skimming the incoming waves. There was no sign of any sort of shipwreck.

Mr Goggles adjusted his trusty glass. "Cap'n, the wreck be manned!"

"A-haar!" whooped the pirates, eager for a brawl.

"Be there many?" asked the captain.

"Aye," said Mr Goggles. "The wreck be a-swarming with pipkins."

"Pipkins?" said Jason, squinting again. Now, he could see the cross of a mast. It was flying the Jolly Roger.

"All change, please!" the driver called, beginning to bring the bus to a halt.

"Be they armed?" asked the captain, more concerned with the prospect of battle.

The reply came back, "They be wielding strange-looking cutlasses, Cap'n. They be swinging them round their toes."

The bus pulled into a stop and Jason at last caught sight of the 'wreck'. "That's not a proper shipwreck," he groaned.

"I be seeing it!" Mr Candle squeaked, bouncing in his seat like a happy rabbit. "It be there among coves and strange green beaches!"

"That's a crazy golf course!" Jason cried. "You can't storm that!"

But with a thunder of clogs, the pirates, including Scuttle, had gone.

Chapter Nineteen

The sea front was busy with afternoon traffic. There were several blared horns and squealing brakes as the pirates dodged the steady stream of cars. Jason wisely took the pelican crossing. But by the time he had managed to cross the road, the pirates had already invaded the golf course and were causing mayhem on the outer holes. An irate attendant stepped out of his kiosk. "Oi! You lot! It's two pounds fifty each for adults!"

"It's no good," panted Jason, tugging the man's sleeve. "They're real pirates. They want your treasure." He pointed to Mr Scabb who was digging his hook into the top of a barrel and trying to lift it off the ground.

"They'll have a job," the attendant muttered. "All the trimmings are set in concrete."

Just then a young boy cried. "Oi, Mister! Gimme my club."

Jason looked up. Captain Blackhead was aboard the broken ship (in reality, hole number nine) swishing his new found 'sword' through the air. "I be taking this ship, salt 'n' all!" he cried.

Salt 'n' all! echoed Swivel, fluttering on to a plastic gravestone (which told the story of One-eyed Bill, who'd be a pirate still, if he hadn't eaten a bucket of swill).

By now, a small crowd was beginning to gather. They were pointing at the pirates and snapping pictures. A queue had formed at the kiosk window. "Crikey," the attendant said, "look at the business your mates are bringing in."

"They're not my mates," Jason said tiredly. "I'm looking for one with a pimple and an eye patch. Have you seen him? He might look like a dog."

Just then, Jason spotted Scuttle by hole number eighteen. He was deep in conversation with a group of children. The pirate had a bright yellow golf ball in his hand. "You be telling this true?" he asked. "If I be dropping this ball in the nogget the cannon be a-firing and I be claiming treasure?"

"Yes," said the children. One of them handed him a club.

Scuttle studied the task. The 'nogget' (the hole) was at the top of a sloping piece of baize. The ball had to be knocked through a tricky little zig-zag of wooden blocks to reach it. The slightest inaccuracy in the shot and the ball would be lost and the game over. To prevent any chance of cheating, the hole was protected by a perspex cover. This proved no barrier to Scuttle. With a quick look round to make sure that none of his shipmates were watching, he turned into a dog, grabbed the ball in his mouth, pushed his snout up under the perspex and spat the ball down the hole.

The cannon fired.

The children cheered.

And the pirates, thinking they were under attack, stormed the attendant's kiosk.

Even while his captors were trying to subdue him the attendant was trying to negotiate terms. "I'll pay all of you twenty quid a week, plus tips. Extra if you pose for holiday snaps. How much do you want for the parrot? That performing dog's a must. Come on, lads, you won't get a deal like this in Filey."

"Where be your treasure?" Mr Floggem sneered.

The attendant shrugged. "Fire the cannon, you get a free round of golf." The captain grabbed the attendant's ear. "All right," the man squealed, "we'll make it a round at The Dancing Fish. Nineteenth hole. You can't say fairer than that."

"Where be The Dancing Fish?" growled the captain.

The attendant nodded in the direction of the beach.

Beyond a stall selling rock and postcards and candyfloss the prow of a boat was just visible.

Jason, hiding with Scuttle round the back of the kiosk, gasped in surprise. So there *was* a boat. He gave the seadog a nudge with his knee. "Come on, quick, while they're nicking all the golf balls. This is our chance to leg it."

"I be boggled," yapped the seadog, turning a circle. "It be right mutinous to run with you. That be the plank for sure."

"If you don't come with me," Jason said tautly, "you'll be gnawing old bones for the rest of your days."

The seadog pondered this option a moment. "If it be coddled with seaweed and spit, an old bone or two be tasty," he muttered. "I be right partial to old bone stew."

"Come on-nn," growled Jason. "We've got to *go*."

Before the dog could argue further, Jason grabbed him by the scruff of the neck and hauled him away. They slipped past a cabin hiring out deckchairs and hurried across the open promenade – unaware that the ever-observant Mr Goggles was on the lookout...

"Cap'n, I be spying the boy heading for the boat."

The captain narrowed his gaze. "Where be that toothpick Scuttle?"

Mr Goggles looked again. "Cap'n, the boy hast spake the spell! The lad be followed by the mangy cur!"

"Treachery!" the pirates cried.

"Durr, they be running for the stone," said Mr Scabb (even he could work that one out).

"Aar," growled the captain. "BE AFTER THEM, LADS!"

By the rock stall, Jason heard the shout and realised he had to do something, fast. Suddenly, he spotted the perfect diversion. Just along the pavement was a large yellow plastic container. Imprinted on the side was the word SALT. In wintry weather the salt would be sprinkled across the road to melt any ice and stop cars skidding. Now it would be used to stop pirates in their tracks.

"Captain! I've found your treasure!" Jason shouted. He dashed to the bin and flipped the lid.

Swivel immediately arched his wings. *Grains o' salt!*

The pirates, unable to resist their curse, swooped on the bin like a flock of vultures.

Jason had to grab Scuttle hard by the ears and use both hands to tug him away.

"But there be salt there, boy," the seadog whimpered.

"Yeah, but look what's here," said Jason, spinning the pirate about.

Ahead of them, set in a bed of gravel, with old breakwaters built in all around, lay a handsome wooden boat. It was 'moored' (by an anchor on a rusted chain) well below street level, touching the edge of the beach itself. It was more like a barge than a pirate ship, which probably explained why Jason had never noticed it before. It had no masts or rigging of any kind, and all that protruded from the row of gun ports were curtains flickering in the stiff sea breeze. At the rear of the ship was a large poop deck, which looked to be some sort of function room. It was accessed by a staggered flight of steps, bearing a sign saying: Gangplank Bar. The main entrance was straight ahead – two portholed doors, cut into the hull at the base of the stern. The wings of the doors were trimmed with seashells and decked with paintings of jolly-faced pirates. Either side of the paintings were two large cannons, beautifully-polished and lovingly restored. Above the door, written to look like a wave, were the words The Dancing Fish.

"We made it," breathed Jason, grinning in triumph. "We got to the tavern. Look up there."

He pointed to a pole jutting out at an angle above the main doors. A flag was hanging limply around it.

Suddenly a gust of wind got up, catching the flag and making it flap. A blue fish danced on a bright white background. "Yes," cried Jason, punching the air. "Bet that's made your eyes light up."

"Aye," said the dog, with a dizzy blink.

His eyes had indeed lit up. That strange glazed look had entered them again.

His pupils were as white as two full moons.

Chapter Twenty

"Right," said Jason, catching his breath. "First we'll find Dad, then you can—"

"Come, boy," the seadog cut in sharply. "There be no time for idle yarns." He sniffed the ground and padded stealthily towards the entrance.

"All right, but let me do the talking," said Jason, moving quickly to get in front of the dog. He gulped. He wouldn't normally be allowed in a pub unaccompanied, but this was an emergency. He put his shoulder to the left-hand door. It swung open with a welcoming creak. Scuttle slipped inside. For a moment the dog was bathed in a soft green spotlight angling down from a wooden beam. Then he was away, weaving through tables, sniffing at the floor for all he was worth.

Jason turned towards the bar. Two men were working

behind it. Both were wearing light blue sweatshirts with a motif of a pirate ship stitched on the arm. One of them, a young man with pony-tailed hair, was punching an order into the till. The other was drying glasses with a teatowel. Jason headed for that end of the bar.

"Yes, son? What can I do for you?"

The man with the tea towel tossed it aside. It landed by a sink, foaming with bubbles.

"I'm looking for my dad – Mr Webberly. Is he here?"

The barman turned to his mate. "Jim, where's Brian Webberly gone?"

The pony-tailed barman closed the till. "Bookies, to collect a bet, I think. He can't be long. That's his drink just there."

Jason glanced at the half pint of beer, sitting vacantly on the bar.

"You must be Jason?" the older barman asked. He put his hands on the bar and straightened his arms. Tattoos rippled over his muscles. On his sweatshirt he had a name badge: Fred. "We've heard a lot about you today. Your dad's been telling us you're fond of pirates."

"Sort of," Jason nodded, anxiously wondering where the seadog had got to. On the far side of the pub was a man playing a fruit machine; in the corner, a couple were holding hands. Two pool cues lay against a cushion

159

of the table. The pub was virtually empty.

"Here, what do you think of this?" asked Fred. With a swish, he wrapped a bar towel round his head, closed one eye and did his best to *haar* like a pirate. "Be you liking life aboard The Dancing Fish?" He stamped his right foot on to a stool and slapped his thigh like a pantomime prince.

"Is this a proper boat?" Jason asked.

Fred grinned and shook his head. "It's what's called a theme pub, son, built around the legend of the Skegness pirates." He beckoned Jason close and in a hushed voice said, "Some folks say this stuff on display came off a boat called *The Slippery Skeggle*. Now that *was* a real pirate ship."

He pointed over Jason's shoulder. All around the upper walls of the pub were various examples of piratey icons: cutlasses; pistols; rope and rigging; black-hooped shirts; a three-cornered hat; a cat-o'-nine-tails; a hook; a peg leg; a string of pearls (false presumably); a spade; several maps and...

"What's that?" asked Jason, coming full circle back to the bar. He pointed to a wooden display case, fixed high on the wall above the upturned spirit bottles. There was something behind the glass-fronted door, but he couldn't see what.

"Ah, that's our pride and joy," said Fred. He reached

under the bar and flicked a switch. The case filled with a lustrous blue light.

Inside was a shimmering stone.

"Hhh!" gasped Jason, stumbling back. "Is that the—?"

"Hey, there's a dog in here," said Jim. He was over by the open end of the bar.

"Dog?" said Fred, turning to see.

"Someone's sent it in for a joke," Jim laughed. "It's got a scarf on its head, bit like a—" With a wallop he jumped back into the bar, knocking an ice bucket off the counter. He paled as if he'd seen a ghost.

He hadn't; he'd seen a dog change into a pirate.

"Oh heck," gasped Fred. "Not another."

"Another?" said Jason as Scuttle leapt on to a table, then sprang on to the bar itself.

Two glasses and an ashtray hit the floor. The smooching couple upped and left. The man at the fruit machine abandoned his nudges.

"Scuttle, what are you doing?" Jason hissed. This wasn't part of the plan. The pirate seemed to be out of control. It was just as if being close to the stone had switched on some hidden force inside him. Jason leapt back with a start. Of course. That was exactly right. Scuttle was responding to a deep-seated spell. He was 'sniffing out' the stone like Aunt Hester had said. He was going through with his task!

"Jim, fetch the boss," Fred said calmly.

Jim backed away up a flight of stairs.

Scuttle stamped a belligerent clog. "I BE A FEARSOME SEADOG!" he rasped. "STAND BY TO BE BOARDED!"

Fred readied himself for action. "Jason, stay out of the way," he cautioned. "There's going to be a spot of trouble."

Scuttle pounded along the bar.

"It's all right. I know him," Jason said. He tried to take hold of Scuttle's ankle.

Mr Scuttle shook the boy off.

"Jason, stand back," Fred said loudly. "I know what this character's after."

Scuttle fixed his moon-eyed gaze on the display case, his eyes dizzy with salty desire. "THE STONE BE MINE!" he bellowed, and launched himself to the back of the bar.

"Right, letsbeavingyerthen!" Fred shouted, and took Scuttle down in a flying tackle.

Both men hit the floor with a thump.

For a moment all that Jason could hear were the bumps and thuds of the two men wrestling. Then Fred's voice said, "What the devil?" and a wiry-haired terrier leapt on to the bar. Scuttle had changed his form mid-fight and had wriggled free of the other man's grasp. He set his gaze on the saltstone again and prepared to spring.

At that moment a soft voice said, "Hey, doggie, you like these, yes?"

Jason gasped in astonishment. "Mr Poppal! What are *you* doing here?" The chip-shop owner stepped into the bar from the stairs which led to the private quarters. He had a bag of pork scratchings in his hand and was shaking them at Scuttle, inviting him to take one.

"He's the boss," said Fred, getting to his feet. "This is one of his pubs."

Mr Poppal raised a hand to acknowledge Jason's question. "I followed you, my friend, all the way from Leicester. We see to this doggie, then we talk."

Scuttle by now had postponed his leap, caught in two minds between the lure of the saltstone and the bag of pork scratchings.

Mr Poppal popped a scratching into his mouth. "Ah, beautifully salty," he said. "You try some, doggie pirate?"

Scuttle hopped from one paw to the other.

Mr Poppal spilled some scratchings on to the bar. One skittered right between Scuttle's paws. The temptation proved too much. Scuttle bent his head to take the food...

…and Fred and Mr Poppal pounced.

"Treachery!" barked the dog as the men overpowered him. "I be terrible tricked. Stand to me, boy!"

Jason, unsure of whose side he ought to be on, said: "You're not going to hurt him are you, Mr Poppal?"

Mr Poppal staggered back with Scuttle in his arms. "We take him to the cellar, Jase. Have to lock him in. Steer the ship, my friend. Two minutes. No more. Old Poppa explain to you then."

Jason bit his lip and nodded.

Fred opened a trapdoor in the floor. With Mr Poppal's help, he bundled the seadog down a set of stairs and pulled the trap flat with a shuddering bang.

The impact reverberated round the pub.

Above the bar, the saltstone casing tilted. Jason held his breath. Was it going to fall?

Yes.

With a creak, the casing slid down the wall, clipped the mirrored tiles and tumbled over. Jason sprinted round the bar. Miraculously, the case was still intact, only its catch had come unhooked. The saltstone lay unbroken on the floor. Jason bent down and picked it up.

It felt surprisingly cold to the touch; much lighter than Jason had anticipated, too. He wondered if it might be like a sponge, perforated inside by a honeycomb of tunnels? In shape it reminded him of the Isle of Wight, which he'd had to draw once for a Geography project. He brought it close to his nose and sniffed. The powerful scent of the untamed sea immediately made his nostrils tingle. When he held it to his ear he fancied he could just hear the rush of the tide, foaming along a sandy shore.

He turned the stone carefully through his fingers. The spiky, irregular, smooth-faced crystals blinked like a set of fairy lights. For a moment he remembered Aunt Hester's voice, croaking away in the back of his mind: *the stone has strange effects on* boys. Jason allowed himself a nonchalant shrug. The stone seemed pretty harmless to him. But he didn't really care much about its powers. All that mattered was finishing the task. Scuttle had bungled it. And Mr Poppal and Fred were still in the cellar. Now the chance had come his way. He told himself he wasn't going to fluff it.

A-haar, he whispered like a looting pirate, and slipped the saltstone under his T-shirt.

Now it belonged to him.

Chapter Twenty One

As Jason was tucking his T-shirt in, the doors to the pub swung open again. A whistling figure wandered in. Strangely, Jason found himself wishing for a cutlass. He looked briefly at the swords on the wall, shook the thought from his mind and hurried round the bar to head the figure off. He was relieved to find it was only his dad.

Mr Webberly raised a surprised eyebrow. "Jason! What are you doing here? Get bored at the house, then, did you?"

Jason opened his mouth to respond, but somehow the words wouldn't form on his tongue.

His father just smiled and tousled his hair. "It's quiet in here. Where is everyone?"

Against his better wishes Jason heard himself rasp, "They all be abandoning ship."

"Pardon?" Mr Webberly said.

Jason blinked and looked a bit puzzled. "They be gone," he muttered, tapping his head with the heel of his palm. "It be an order from Mr Fred."

Mr Webberly smiled and took a sip of his drink. "Been telling you a few tall tales, has he?"

"There be a trickerous tale to tell," said Jason…if only he could find the right way to tell it. His tongue seemed to have gained a life of its own.

Mr Webberly eased himself on to a stool. "Where *is* Fred? Changing a barrel?"

Jason had the answer to that straight off: "He be in the cellar with the mangy cur!"

Mr Webberly leaned backwards and peered at the trapdoor. "Are you and Fred playing a game or something? Why are you talking so strangely?"

"I not be furzackerly knowing," said Jason. And this was not a lie. Every time he tried to say something sensible his words were coming out in pirate speak. He shifted the saltstone round his waist. It was pulsing gently against his skin, making his midriff itch.

Mr Webberly, seeing him scratching, said: "You haven't caught fleas off that dog, I hope?"

Mention of Scuttle sent a mild surge of anger through Jason's body. "That cur be hopping better than a flea when I be stamping my clog on his toe!"

Mr Webberly cast his eyes downwards. "Jason, you've got your trainers on. You've never worn a clog in your life."

That didn't stop Jason crying, "A-haar!" and dancing a quick hornpipe.

Mr Webberly drummed his fingers on the bar. "Jason, why *are* you here? Is everything all right at the house?"

Quick, tell him, Jason's real mind badgered, *tell him now that Mum and Kim are in trouble.* Jason concentrated hard and spat the words out: "There be a strange predicament at Shingle Towers!"

Mr Webberly furrowed his brow. "Am I to understand you've been naughty, Jason? Have you upset Aunt Hester?"

"Aye!" said Jason with a buccaneering wink. "The Skegglewitch be more narked than a noggin!"

"Well it's nothing to be proud of," his father said, adopting a sterner look. "Has your mother sent you here?"

Jason banged a fist down hard on the bar top. "Nay, Dadkin. I not be dispatched in a mumly manner. I be sent by the witch to plunder and pillage. That be the rub of it. Aar." He flicked a pork scratching into the air and crunched it noisily as it entered his mouth. Under his T-shirt, the saltstone throbbed.

Mr Webberly shook his head in despair. "I think you'd better tell me what this is about."

There was nothing Jason would have liked to do more. But for the moment he had a rather pressing problem. The pork scratching had left him with a raging thirst. He glanced at his father's unfinished shandy. "I be drier than a dusty dog in a desert!" And he glugged the shandy down in one swig, splashing most of it over his face. He slammed the empty glass on the bar and belched.

"Right," said Mr Webberly, folding his arms. "It's not often I'm forced to censure you, Jason, but this time you've gone a little too—"

Thunka. Thunka. Thunka.

"Silence!" hissed Jason. "What be that thunking?" He turned his face to the stern of the boat. Someone had gone running up the gangplank stairs.

"The wind I should think," Mr Webberly replied. "Those stairs rattle when it gets a bit blustery. Now, as I was saying, it's not very clever acting up when—"

Thubba. Thubba. Thubba.

Jason turned again. "There be thubbings, too!" A figure had just flashed past the window. A figure in a blousy shirt.

Jason snatched a bar-towel off a pump and tied it

quickly round his head. He snatched up another and threw it at his dad. "Man the guns. We be under attack!"

Mr Webberly patiently folded the towel and dropped it on to the bar top again. "Jason, I'm going to count to five and then this nonsense is going to stop. One… (Jason leapt over the bar) two… (he stamped an urgent foot on the trap door), three… (a parrot landed on Mr Webberly's shoulder) four… (the parrot cried, *Grains o' salt!*)". Mr Webberly swallowed hard. "Erm, dare I say…"

The doors to the pub barged open.

STAND BY TO BE BOARDED! a rough voice yelled.

Mr Webberly cleared his throat. "…five?" he gulped.

Chapter Twenty Two

Mr Scabb and Mr Blue Thumb thundered in, knocking tables over in their wake. Mr Goggles dropped in through a narrow skylight and landed, clog-perfect, on the centre of the pool table. Mr Floggem dived through an open window, tumbling like an acrobat across the floor. It was a clever, dramatic, well organised attack. Jason clenched his teeth. He had little choice for now but to duck down and hide.

Mr Webberly on the other hand roared with laughter. "Ha! Now I get it. Well done, Jason. You had me going there, all right. Don't tell me, Fred's been planning this for months? Which of these jolly Tars *is* Fred? Ah, this'll be him in the hat."

Captain Blackhead swept in. Seeing that the ship had been claimed at no loss, he lifted a fist and cried, *A-haar!*

A-haar! roared the crew.

Arrk! went Swivel and landed on the bar among the pork scratchings, spilling one over the edge. *Grains o' salt!* he reported.

Jason tightened with fear. If the pirates went for the scratchings now he would be spotted with ease and the game would be up. But the pirates, full to their kerchiefs with salt, had no desire for scratchings. They were far more taken with Brian Webberly than any squawkings from the pestersome parrot.

Mr Webberly shook a jolly fist. "Yo, ho, ho! What tide brings you to these shores, Mr Fred? Fabulous beard, by the way."

Mr Floggem and the captain exchanged a glance. "It be a gribbling tide for you," said Blackhead. He gazed around the pub and scratched his whiskers. A tiny piece of frog spawn slithered out. "Where be the rest of your crew?"

Jason tensed as the trapdoor opened a crack. Mr Poppal peeked out. He caught Jason's eye. *How many?* he mouthed.

Jason held up six fingers.

Mr Poppal nodded. The trapdoor closed.

Mr Webberly stood to attention and boldly declared the state of his crew. "I'm afraid it's just me and my boy, Mr Fred – well, I *did* have a boy. He seems to have left me to face the music. Love the costume. Pongs a bit, mind."

"Gag it, you villainous toad," hissed Jason. He grimaced and hotched towards the sink. Beneath his T-shirt, the saltstone was almost burning his skin.

Captain Blackhead picked up a beer mat and held it against Mr Webberly's throat. "I be anxiously seeking *a cur and a boy*. Mr Goggles be spying them hastening this way."

Mr Webberly pretended to gibber. "Flipping heck, Jase. I think we're for the plank!"

"Aye," sneered Mr Floggem, "that be so."

Behind the bar, the trapdoor creaked.

Mr Webberly stood his ground. "Tell them nothing, Jason. Name, rank and serial number, that's all they get. Stiff upper lip. We're from Leicester, remember."

"Avast!" roared Blackhead. He hurled the beer mat aside.

"A vast what?" said Mr Webberly. "Oh, you mean 'stop'."

"Take him!" cried the captain.

Mr Scabb leapt forward and twisted Mr Webberly's arm behind his back.

"Ooh! Ow! Ooh! Now, come on, chaps. I say, watch what you're doing with that hook! This is taking it a bit far, isn't it? OK, Fred, I've got the message. Just rattle your charity tins and I'll pop a quid in each. I—"

With a bang, the trapdoor blasted open. Mr Poppal came fast up the stairs, pushing Scuttle (now in his pirate form) in front of him. Mr Poppal had Scuttle held in an armlock. As they cleared the cellar, Fred sneaked out. Keeping low and out of sight, he tracked sideways along the bar to Jason.

"Good lad, stay right where you are," he whispered, as the pirates, glad of some true opposition, roared into action. Through the mirrored tiles Jason saw Mr Goggles leap on to a table and tear a cutlass off the wall. He threw it across the room to his captain. Blackhead caught it and whirled it through his hands.

"Captain, stay your hand," said Mr Poppal. "As you see, I have one of your crew."

"Good Lord! Mr Poppal!" Mr Webberly exclaimed.

Mr Scabb immediately tightened his armlock, making Mr Webberly howl.

Jason, hearing his father's torment, cracked his knuckles and growled to Fred: "I be making them pay right dearly for that."

"Shush," whispered Fred. "Let the boss keep them— eh, what did you say?"

Jason quickly retied a shoelace and checked that his beer-towel was still in place. "I be having a cunning plan," he said.

174

"*What?*" said Fred. "What are you talking about?"

Jason slanted his gaze towards the sink. A bottle of washing-up liquid was standing beside it…

Meanwhile, on the opposite side of the bar, Mr Poppal was doing his best to negotiate. "I propose an exchange of men, Captain Blackhead. This pirate, he is rather special, is he not?"

"Mr Scuttle be a treacherous wart," growled the captain. "You be right welcome to him." He brought his cutlass down on a table. The cutlass snapped in two. The blade went flying through the air. It narrowly missed Swivel and rebounded into the well of the bar. Jason grinned. The blade was only plastic. He checked the mirrored tiles again. He could just make out Mr Poppal's face. The boss was looking confused.

"I think you jest me, Captain? This pirate, he storm my tavern alone. You ask me to believe he is not your finest?"

"He be on a charge for desertion," cried the captain, throwing the hilt of the cutlass aside. A murmur carried around the crew.

"That's it, boss, get them unsettled," muttered Fred.

"Aye," said Jason. "We be skirmishing soon."

Fred gripped the boy by the shoulders. "Jason, these characters are dangerous. You're to stay put and do *nothing*, son."

"Cap'n, be taking this flintlock!" cried a voice.

Jason gazed into the mirrors once more. Mr Goggles was raiding the weaponry again. He tore a pistol off the wall and threw it to his captain. The captain pointed at Swivel and fired.

Arrk! went Swivel, taking flight. But all that came his way was a muffled click.

"Cod 'n' bones," moaned the captain. He tossed the gun aside.

Mr Poppal pushed Scuttle closer. There was sweat on the old man's forehead now. "Come, Captain. The trade is fair. This is not your boat, and we are not your enemy. My man for yours. Make the trade and then we talk. You will not succeed in a battle, my friend. I have already sent out word for more men."

With a bang, the front doors opened again. Mr Candle swept in with a captive. "Cap'n, I be taking this hairy swain. He be skulking about the upper deck."

Behind the bar Fred gritted his teeth. "Drat, they've got Jim."

"'Tis time," said Jason, pushing up his sleeves. "When I be giving the order, Mr Fred, you be taking the westerly approach." He pointed to the batwing doors at the opposite end of the bar.

Fred turned to look. In doing so he noticed the wooden display case, lying open on the floor. His gaze switched quickly to the hook on the wall. "Jason, where's the stone?"

"I be taking the gobbet as pickings," said Jason and snatched the washing-up liquid off the sink. He pushed himself into a crouching position.

Meanwhile, Captain Blackhead had tired of his parley with Mr Poppal. "Mr Floggem, be seizing them both!" he commanded.

Mr Poppal, knowing the talking was done, drove Scuttle into Mr Floggem's path. The two pirates collided and crunched to the floor. Mr Poppal spilled a table in front of Mr Blue Thumb and sped towards Jason's dad.

Hearing the commotion, Jason gave his order. "STAND BY TO BE BOARDED!"

"Flipping heck," murmured Fred, "you're a gutsy one all right. Come on, then!" he cried. "Who'sforritfirst?!!" Roaring like a bear, he leapt over the bar.

Jason clambered over and hurried to his dad. "Dadkin, be hasty. Run for it. You be much needed at Shingle Towers."

"Jason, what on earth is going on?"

Jason ducked as a pint glass whizzed through the air and smashed to pieces on a beam behind him. "I be a fearsome seadog, Dadkin. Take leave. I must be joining the skirmish."

"Jason?!"

But Jason, the fearsome seadog had gone, pounding across the table tops as if they were flagstones in the garden lawn. All around him, bodies tangled in combat. Jason ignored them and hurried to his target: Captain Blackhead.

He had paid enough attention in History to remember that capturing the opponents' leader was halfway to winning the battle. The captain was strutting about, ordering his men to "be fighting like crabs". Jason homed in stealthily, his washing-up bottle primed and at the ready. He thumped on to the final table, held the bottle two-handed at arm's length and splayed his legs to steady his aim.

"Be surrendering, a-haar!"

The captain whirled around. "'Tis you! The scurvy boy."

"Silence, fuzzy face," Jason snarled. He pointed the bottle at the captain's chest.

"What weaponry be this?"

"Bubblings," said Jason with a confident smirk.

The captain gave a start.

"Be giving the order, now," said Jason, and stamped his foot to show he meant business.

That was the moment his daring came unstuck. Or

rather, his *T-shirt* came unstuck. The movement of his leg loosed the hem from his waist and...

Clunk.

The saltstone dropped like a salted egg.

Grains o' salt! cried Swivel, and *everyone* came charging after the treasure.

None arrived quicker than Mr Scuttle.

"A-haar! The gobbet be mine!" he cried, sweeping the stone into his hands at last.

"No!" yelled Jason. "Give it back!" His hands squeezed round the washing-up bottle.

Squuush! Squuush! Squuush! Three squirts of lemon-fresh Twinkle jetted out of the nozzle.

In the blink of an eye Mr Scuttle clamped the saltstone between his teeth and *whoosh!* turned into a dog. The squirts of Twinkle missed him completely and splatted into the captain's chest. But as the seadog turned to scuttle away, he collided hard with a table leg and knocked himself dizzy, spilling the saltstone on to the floor.

The advancing pirates skidded to a halt. Mr Blue Thumb, who was nearest, sniffed the air with caution. "BUBBLINGS!" he reported. "The boy be firing bubblings!"

"I be hit," muttered the captain, and promptly passed out.

The pirates gasped and cowered away.

"That's right," gulped Jason, shaking like a leaf. "I've got washing-up liquid…and I know how to squirt it! Get back, all of you! Put your hands on your heads and…and…your fingers up your noses!"

"Eh?" said Mr Webberly. "Is that possible?"

"They know what I mean!" Jason shouted. He flipped the bottle. The pirates skittered back.

Fred hurried to Jason's side. "Good lad," he said, stooping to pick the saltstone up. He whipped the towel off Jason's head and wrapped the saltstone up in it. "Keep them covered, Jase. Jim and the boss'll do the rest." Mr Poppal, aided by Jim, was ushering the pirates into a corner.

"What about him?" Jason swung his bottle at Scuttle.

"I be boggled," yapped the seadog, staggering about. An egg-shaped bump had come up on his head.

"Squirt him if he tries any funny stuff," said Fred. "I'm just going to count them. Didn't you say there were six pirates besides the dog? 'Cos I can only see—"

Suddenly, the doors of the pub almost crashed off their hinges. Mr Candle powered in, rolling a cannon.

"A-haar!" cried the pirates, shaking their fists.

"Good grief!" cried Mr Webberly. "You can't fire that in here!"

Mr Candle grinned as if he knew better. "I be finding

180

this handy fire stick," he said. He flicked the wheel on a cigarette lighter. A jet of flame nearly singed his eyebrows. He held the lighter over the cannon's fuse.

"We be trumping your bubblings!" the pirates cried.

"They're bluffing. They haven't any ammo," said Fred.

Mr Candle delved into his pockets. He pulled out a handy supply of golf balls. His shipmates grinned and did the same.

"Be surrendering!" Mr Floggem growled. "Or Mr Candle be blasting you to bibbles!"

Mr Poppal grimaced and took a pace back. Slowly, he raised his hands. He nodded at Fred to do the same.

Fred nudged Jason with his knee. "Sorry, son, they've got us cold. Those cannons work."

Jason gulped and dropped his washing-up liquid.

The pirates stomped forward. Mr Blue Thumb kicked the Twinkle out of the way. Mr Scabb took Scuttle by the scruff of the neck and held him up for Mr Floggem. Mr Floggem, who had clearly assumed command while the captain was out for the count, whipped the kerchief off Scuttle's head. "Mr Scuttle be a servant of the witch," he sneered. "He be in league with the boy and these toads."

"Aye!" roared the crew. "Toads they be!"

Mr Floggem glowered at Fred. "I reckon you be having our treasure."

Fred sighed and handed the saltstone over.

The pirate carefully unwrapped it. The saltstone, sitting on its towel bed, twinkled like the embers of a strange white fire.

"You've got to let me have that back," pleaded Jason.

"Avast," Mr Floggem barked. "This be our trade for *The Slippery Skeggle*. Mr Scabb, be throwing these curs in the hold. I fancy we be letting them rest awhile, afore they stretch their legs."

"Stretch our legs?" asked Mr Webberly. "Are we going for a walk?"

"Aye," said Mr Floggem, grinning like a snake. "It be a goodly walk to the end of a plank."

Chapter Twenty Three

"Well, my friends, we find ourselves in a modest pickle." Mr Poppal took off his spectacles and rubbed them against the sleeve of his shirt.

"Pickle?" Mr Webberly snorted. "I'd say it's more like gherkin jam. It's flipping cold in here too."

"It *is* a cellar," said Jason, rubbing his arms. He tapped an aluminium barrel. It responded with a hollow clonk.

"Don't panic, I'll soon have us out," said Fred. He beckoned Jason over to a large wooden ramp that sloped upwards towards the far wall of the cellar. "When we have beer delivered, the brewery roll the barrels down this chute. Those doors up there open straight into the car park." He pointed to another access hatch built into the wall at the top of the ramp. The doors of the hatch were bolted shut and secured at their centre by a padlocked hasp. "If we can prise the padlock, we're free."

Jim pulled a penknife out of his pocket. "I reckon I can lever the screws from that hasp."

Fred patted his shoulder. "Quick as you can."

Jim stepped on to a crate and set to work. Fred and Jason rejoined the others, all of whom were perched on barrels. Swivel (who'd been thrown into the cellar for good measure) was sitting on Mr Poppal's shoulder, quietly preening his glossy feathers.

Mr Webberly raised a questioning finger. "Can someone explain to me what is going on? Where did all these pirates come from? I thought they fizzled out years ago?"

Jason took a breath and said to his father: "Dad, Aunt Hester's an evil witch."

Mr Webberly's face tightened into a frown. "Jason, I strongly advise you not to let your mother hear you talk like that."

"Dad, I'm not kidding. Aunt Hester's the Skegglewitch. She wants to become the Queen of the Seas. She's been keeping the pirates in bottles in her cellar. Scuttle came out of that one I smashed. She's made Mum her maid and turned Kim to a pebble. If she doesn't get the saltstone by high tide tonight she's going to throw Kimberley on to the beach and let the sea just wash her away."

Mr Webberly folded his arms and eyed his son very carefully indeed. "Jason, have they been giving you special fantasy homework at school or something? You haven't had an author in again, have you?"

At this point, Mr Poppal intervened. "My friend, I think you should take the boy seriously. Here is your proof, after all." He opened a palm towards Scuttle. "You witnessed his change from a pirate, did you not?"

Mr Webberly chewed his lip. "I assumed I'd had one drink too many."

"A pint and a half of shandy?" said Jim. There was a clatter as he forced the first screw from the hasp.

"Show him," said Jason. He kicked Scuttle's barrel.

"Blubber 'n' bones," the seadog grumbled. With a whoosh he turned himself into a man, shouted a rather lacklustre a-haar, danced on his barrel then became a dog again.

Mr Webberly turned a delicate shade of grey. "Well, Jason, all I can say is next time you decide to bring a stray dog home can you make it a normal one, please."

"You brought him to Leicester," Jason protested.

"How do you work that out?"

"Aunt Hester put his bottle in your jacket, Dad. It

was her sneaky way of sending him to this pub. She knows you always come here."

"So what went wrong?" asked Fred. "Your dad was definitely here last weekend."

Everyone looked at Mr Webberly. Jason's dad began to think back. "Oh dear," he muttered, blushing profusely. "*I* was here, but my jacket wasn't. I parked outside the bookies and walked from there. I left my jacket in the boot of the car."

"There you have it," Mr Poppal said nodding. "The pirate was posted, but not delivered."

Before anyone could comment, a beer pump whirred into life. Jason turned to see a spurt of amber-coloured liquid go racing through a line of plastic tubing. In the body of the pub, a bottle broke.

"Sounds like they're living it up," said Fred as the cellar shivered its ancient timbers to raucous belts of back-slapping laughter and the thunderous clatter of dancing clogs.

"The crew be making merry," said Scuttle, "afore they lay the plank."

Jason's shoulders stiffened with fear.

"Jason," Mr Poppal inquired calmly. "Tell us, quickly, if you will, all that took place at Shingle Towers. If we are to save your mother and sister we need your information, my friend."

So Jason took a breath and gabbled everything out, right from meeting Scuttle in the park all the way through to his deal with Aunt Hester. (What he didn't mention, with Scuttle in attendance, was anything about *The Slippery Skeggle* being turned to splinters if the pirates failed to return the stone.)

At the end Mr Webberly turned to him and said, "You mean to say this whole ballyhoo is all because of that lump of rock?"

"Dad, the saltstone's a powerful gobbet. How did you find it, Mr Poppal?"

"DONE IT!" cried Jim. He tore off the hasp and hurled it to the floor.

Fred stomped up the ramp and banged the hatch doors open. A window of dusky sky appeared. "Jason. Come on, you're first!" he said. He wiggled the fingers of his outstretched hand.

Mr Poppal turned Jason by the shoulders. "Go. I explain the story of the stone to you later."

Jason ran to the ramp. He clamped hands with Fred and was hauled up in one.

"I be next," yapped Scuttle. He scrambled up without anyone's help.

Mr Webberly went third, then Fred, then Jim. Swivel

flapped through with ease. When it came to Mr Poppal's turn, however, there was a gap of several seconds. Jason knelt anxiously beside the hatch. Deep within the pub he could hear the sound of floorboards being ripped up. The pirates were starting to build their plank. "Mr Poppal, come on-nn," he hissed, and peered into the body of the cellar.

Mr Poppal was crouching behind a beer pump. He had a small green holdall in his hand, which he must have had hidden somewhere in the cellar. He pushed an empty stack of beer crates aside, then from the wall behind the crates carefully removed a few loose bricks. He fumbled around in the hole he'd created and brought out three separate objects. Jason didn't see the first. The second appeared to be a plastic bottle of cream-coloured liquid. The third was a large brown leather pouch. It looked old and worn and was tied at the neck by two yellow drawstrings. Was it treasure, perhaps? Mr Poppal's life-savings? Jason had no idea. But the old man wasn't going to leave without it. He pushed the pouch into the holdall along with the other things, zipped it up smartly and climbed the ramp.

"Your car," he said to Jason's dad, shielding his eyes from the afternoon sun. "We take that. It is larger than mine. You, me, Jason and the dog: we go to Shingle Towers."

"I'm parked on the road," Mr Webberly gulped. "We'll have to sneak past the front doors of the pub."

"Mr Poppal, what about the stone?" asked Jason. "We can't go to Shingle Towers without it."

Mr Poppal clamped the holdall under his arm. "Come," he whispered, leading everyone away from the cellar. "We make a diversion – and take the stone."

"That be right cunning," the seadog beamed. But his mood soon changed when he learned the diversion was going to be him.

"Go in, bark, draw them away from the stone," said Mr Poppal.

"Suffering seashells," the seadog quaked.

"Do it," hissed Jason. "Or we might miss the tide."

Scuttle crunkled a lip. He padded warily through the doors.

A few seconds later, the commotion began. Through a window, Jason saw the pirates chasing Scuttle around the tables. *Cap'n, the mangy cur be abroad! The prisoners be gone! The hold be emptied!*

Outside, Mr Poppal took Swivel off his shoulder and ran a finger down the parrot's neck. "Fly, my friend. Find the stone. Bring it."

Arrk! went Swivel and fluttered through the doors.

He had barely been gone ten seconds when Scuttle

came haring out of the pub with several pirates and a cannon on his tail!

"Get going!" cried Fred. "Me and Jim'll hold them off."

Mr Poppal ran for the car, pulling Jason and his dad along with him. Mr Webberly buzzed the locks. Jason dived into the back, leaving his door wide open for Scuttle. The dog leapt in. Jason slammed the door shut. Half a second later the cannon went off. A shower of golf balls sped towards the car. Five whizzed over the roof and bonnet. One thumped into the passenger wing.

"You'd better not have dented that!" yelled Mr Webberly, adding rather tamely, "I'm not sure my insurance covers cannon fire."

"Drive," said Mr Poppal, pointing urgently ahead.

Mr Webberly revved the engine. "Can't, too much traffic." The car rolled back and forth like a tensing rubber band.

"Wait! Swivel's coming!" Jason cried. The bird had just flapped out of the pub and was over the pirates, heading for the car. He had the saltstone in his claws.

"We dare not open a door," breathed Mr Poppal. "They are reloading the gun."

Jason looked back. Mr Poppal was right. Fred and Jim were managing to hold three pirates at bay, but Mr

Candle was free and busily stuffing golf balls down the cannon's barrel.

"Be windward!" yapped Scuttle. "Or we be smithereens and smoke!"

Jason bounced frantically in his seat. "The sun roof!" he cried. He jumped forward and unwound the handle. A rectangle of bright blue sky appeared.

Boom! The cannon roared again. A golf ball crashed against Jason's window, making a spider's web pattern in the glass. *Dunk!* something bounced on the roof of the car. The saltstone tumbled in – along with a shower of grey-green feathers.

"Oh no, Swivel's hit!"

Mr Poppal caught the stone and dropped it in his pocket. Looking up for Swivel he shouted, "It is only his tail! Mr Webberly, make haste!"

With a screech of rubber the car sped away (Swivel clinging to the radio aerial). Jason whipped round and peeked out the back window. In a matter of seconds, The Dancing Fish was just a minor blot on the seascape. Mr Webberly quickly changed gear and the car whizzed away from the lights of the town and took the turn for the old sea road. Jason flopped back in his seat, relieved. "Phew, that was close. Good old Swivel."

Mr Webberly nodded in agreement. "Very brave

under fire, that bird. I must say you've got him well trained, Mr Poppal."

That brought a puzzled frown to Jason's face. "But Swivel belongs to the pirates. How did you make him obey you, Mr Poppal?"

Mr Poppal took a deep and thoughtful breath. "I was kind to the bird when the pirates were not. It is fortunate that Swivel remembers me now."

Mr Webberly glanced across. "Remembers you? But you only just met him."

Mr Poppal looked out across the shimmering sea. His gaze was still fixed on the water as he said, "That is not so. It is time you knew the truth. Please, do not be alarmed." Slowly, he put a hand to his head – and pulled off all his hair.

"Good grief!" cried Mr Webberly, nearly swerving into some cones.

"He be eggy," barked Scuttle. "Shiny as a shell!"

Mr Poppal didn't stop at the hair. He tore the moustache off his lip as well, then removed his spectacles and threw them aside.

"W-who are you?" Jason gulped.

Mr Poppal turned. In a cultured English accent he said, "Three hundred years ago, my friend, the pirates took a prisoner aboard *The Slippery Skeggle*."

"Blistering barnacles!" the seadog barked. With a whoosh he turned himself into a man. "I be knowing your jaunty face!"

Mr Poppal cast a dark-eyed glance at the pirate. "So you should, Mr Scuttle. You were left to guard me once." Mr Poppal slid his gaze towards Jason again. "Yes, my friend, your thoughts are correct. The prisoner aboard *The Skeggle* was me."

Chapter Twenty Four

Mr Webberly spluttered with laughter. "Come off it, Mr Poppal. You're pulling our leg. No one can live for three hundred years!"

"The Skegglewitch has," Jason said nervously. He looked Mr Poppal squarely in the face.

Mr Poppal steepled his fingers. "I am no magician or sorcerer, I assure you, merely an ordinary seafaring man. I have survived by means of tragedy and good fortune. I will tell you what I can of it before we reach the house.

"My name is not Marios Poppalongalot, though you may continue to call me Mr Poppal if you wish. I was born Sebastian Arthur Ffoulkes in the year 1681. My father was a wealthy gentleman. He owned a large portion of land in Lincolnshire. He traded in dry goods and fishing stocks. My family was noble, well-respected.

I grew up a privileged young man.

"At the age of twelve I was sent away to be educated. I returned to these parts at the age of eighteen. It was my father's intention that I should succeed him in the family business. But my passion was not to remain on soil, selling beans and fruit and other commodities. I desired to roam the untamed sea. To challenge her power. To explore her mysteries. That is how I came to learn of the saltstone – and tangled with the Salt Pirates of Skegness."

"Aar," boomed Scuttle.

"Shut up," said Jason, scowling at him. "And don't you try any funny stuff, either." Scuttle had been eyeing Mr Poppal's pocket ever since the stone had gone into it.

Mr Poppal continued, "The stone held a strange fascination for me. Many books I had studied declared it to be the origin of all the salt in the sea. My father, who had profited from trading in salt, often gave thanks to the mythical gem, saying it had paid for our prosperous lifestyle. So, in the year 1701, I determined to set off on a voyage of discovery, to find this fabled jewel. I chartered a ship – a good, strong vessel – to explore the seas around Grubblemuck Island where it was rumoured the stone was hidden. Imagine the horror I felt when, on the final wave of the voyage, I encountered a pirate boat. It was *The Slippery Skeggle*."

"A-haar," went Scuttle under his breath.

"The pirates attacked. My ship was sunk. I, Ffoulkes, was the only survivor. The pirates hauled me aboard, clinging for my life to a barrel of rum. They stripped the rings from my fingers, the shoes from my feet. They even stole the fine blue jacket off my back; the same jacket Captain Blackhead wears to this day. I was blindfolded then and taken to a plank. It was only my wits that saved me from the water. I told Blackhead my father was a wealthy man. I said if the captain spared my life my father would pay a great reward."

"He be offering a handsome ransom," said Scuttle.

"Shut UP!" said Jason and his dad together.

Mr Poppal went on, "Seduced by greed, the pirates threw me in the brig, with barely provisions to feed a mouse. They tied my hands and shaved the hair from my head. Then they set sail for the east coast of England."

Jason gulped and looked out across the marshes. He tried to imagine what life would be like, starving and bound aboard a pirate ship.

Mr Poppal described it for him: "The passage was rough. I did not sleep well. The only company I kept on that difficult voyage were the squealing rats, the creaking timbers and the bird the crew referred to as the pestersome parrot. They placed Swivel with me for stealing maggots from the captain's beard. I shared what food I had with the bird. Without it, he would surely have perished.

"As we sailed, I kept my eyes and ears open. I soon learned to my dismay that the pirates had not only found the stone but planned to exchange it for the witch's treasure. I was determined that should not happen. But I was weak, imprisoned, at the mercy of cut-throats. My situation seemed hopeless.

"Then, one night, as we neared our destination, I heard them arguing about the stone. I knew by now of their affinity for salt and was not surprised to hear that many crewmen desired to keep the gem. Blackhead stabbed his cutlass into the mast. He spoke of his plot to double-cross the witch by only taking her a fragment of stone. Through a crack in the door of the brig, I watched him pound the stone with a club. Two small pieces broke away."

"*Two* pieces?" Jason tugged against his seatbelt.

Mr Poppal nodded. "One piece they took to the witch. The other skittered unseen along the deck and, as fortune would have it, through a rat hole in my door. I used it to cut my bonds, then hid it carefully inside my shirt.

"Then I bided my time. Until the ship was at anchor there was nowhere to escape. But while I waited, I rubbed the stone for comfort. Curiously, after a period of time, I noticed the strength coming back to my limbs. The stone was beginning to invigorate me, in just the same way that Jason told us it brought vitality to Great Aunt Hester. Soon I was fitter than I'd ever been. On the fateful night that the Skegglewitch visited *The Slippery Skeggle*, I made my escape."

"Fuzzlewuck," Scuttle chuntered to himself, grinding his yellow teeth together.

"Did you see her get Scuttle?" Jason asked.

"I saw everything," Mr Poppal replied. "I saw the witch's rage, the cannon being fired. Alas, I could do nothing for Swivel. He was shrunk in the blink of an eye. When Scuttle went too, I knew I must flee. I climbed overboard and dived into the sea. I had swum but twenty strokes when the boat disappeared in a flash of blue light. I was sure it must have exploded, but no splintered hull came drifting past, just a few loose chattels, some of which you saw in The Dancing Fish. I drifted ashore along with the wreckage. I was lucky to be alive."

"I'll say," said Mr Webberly, changing gear. The car

198

zipped past a straw-shedding farm vehicle and zoomed on up the open road. "And the stone has kept you going since 1701?"

"Yes," said Mr Poppal, lacing his fingers. "I quickly discovered that eating the salt in minute quantities stayed the ageing process. Time began to pass slowly for me. Eventually, I inherited my father's wealth. I bought land and properties: taverns, hotels. I prospered, moved around, changed identity often. I watched children grow past me, become old, die. Sometimes, so no one would suspect my secret, I put the stone away and allowed myself to age. But not once did I desire to live for vanity, for the sake of life or the fear of death. I kept myself alive with one thought in mind: to find a means of defeating the witch."

"But why has it taken so long?" asked Jason.

Mr Poppal sighed deeply. "Your aunt has startling powers, Jason. Although by some miracle the stone gave me life, it granted me no further advantage than that. I was mortally afraid of the witch. But I did not stand idle those three hundred years. I studied every scrap of literature I could find, anything relating to the legend of the Skegglewitch. And at last, by a mixture of coincidence and diligence, I discovered her likely weakness."

"What is it?" cried Jason, panting with excitement.

Mr Poppal clutched the holdall tight to his chest. "When the time comes, you will know. For now let it merely be said that your father was a crucial part of this process."

"Me?!" squeaked Mr Webberly, braking sharply to allow a small rabbit to hop across the road. "What did I do?"

Mr Poppal smiled thinly. "You gave us an inside link to Aunt Hester. You came into the pub on your visits to Skegness, often complaining to Fred about the miserable old witch at Shingle Towers. From you we have gathered much vital information."

Jason gave an incredulous frown. "You learned how to beat her – just from Dad moaning?"

Mr Poppal smiled. "Words good or bad can still carry much significance, Jason."

"But if you knew the old bat was a witch," said Mr Webberly, "why didn't you tip us off?"

Mr Poppal tilted his head. "I feared the truth would be too disturbing. So I watched over you a while instead. I bought the chip shop in Leicester, so I might stay close and await developments."

"Developments?" said Jason, almost hiccoughing the word as the car popped over a hump-backed bridge.

Mr Poppal took a breath. "I will explain in a moment.

First let me tell you how I came by the stone."

Jason sat up excitedly. "Did you use sonor equipment, Mr Poppal? Specially trained dolphins? Submarines? Did you have to deep-sea dive for it?"

Mr Poppal laughed and shook his head. "No, my friend, it was far simpler than that. One morning I was out on a fishing trip with Fred when one of the lines began to snag. I carefully reeled it in. Imagine my astonishment when, of all things, this came aboard." He patted his bulging pocket.

"I be taking it fair!" Scuttle demanded. "I be claiming it back. I be—"

"Button it," snapped Jason, wrestling the pirate back into his seat. "Go on, Mr Poppal, what happened next."

"First, I shared my secret with Fred. He is a good and loyal friend. I told him all that you now know and between us we concocted a simple plan to draw the Skegglewitch out of her lair. We put the stone on display in The Dancing Fish and let it be widely known that we had found the mythical gem of the sea. The town soon buzzed with talk of the legend. Tourists flocked like gulls. This was my intention – to spread the gossip. I wanted to entice Aunt Hester with the news, to force her hand, to make her react. I knew she would come for the stone somehow, but her methods were not quite what we expected. Gradually, things began to happen. Freak storms; salt cellars flying about; the sea battering the hull of the pub. Then came the pirate attacks."

Jason and Scuttle sat up smartly.

"Attacks?" said Mr Webberly, stressing the s.

"Yes, my friends. Scuttle was not the first to be sent. Pirates have been storming the pub for months."

Jason quickly thought this through. "They must have been the rest of the crew," he spluttered. "That's why there weren't many bottles in the cellar."

"What be becoming of these men?" jabbered Scuttle.

A grim look set on Mr Poppal's face. Jason guessed the old man had been expecting this question, but did not relish giving the answer. "Each of them tried to pilfer the stone. But we caught them, to a man, and locked them in the cellar. Yet, by dawn, they had always perished."

Jason's mouth turned dry with fear.

"Each turned into a mound of salt."

With a thump, Scuttle promptly passed out.

"A mound of salt?" Mr Webberly repeated.

Mr Poppal nodded dourly. "A cruel and mocking punishment, I fear, for their failure to complete Aunt Hester's task. Scuttle should count himself lucky that his penalty was only to remain a dog. His diversion to Leicester and all it entailed has at least provided him with a second chance. Wake him, Jason. Our destiny is upon us."

Jason looked up. The car had just rolled to a halt, biting gravel beneath its tyres.

They were on the drive of Shingle Towers.

Chapter Twenty Five

Mr Poppal unclipped his belt. He turned and looked solemnly at Jason. "What you are about to witness in this house may curdle the blood in your veins, my friend. But if we are to rid ourselves of this creature we must be prepared to look fear in the face. Trust me and you will come to no harm. Please take this."

He dipped his hand into his pocket and gave Jason the stone.

"Hang on," Mr Webberly protested. "You're not sending Jason in alone?"

Mr Poppal shook his head. "Scuttle goes with him. I will be close at hand. Jason, this is the plan. Do not deviate from these words. You are to give Aunt Hester the stone and humbly beg for your mother and sister to be returned. Keep her talking if you can. That will give me time."

"To do what?" asked Mr Webberly. "What's in that bag?"

Mr Poppal tightened his grip on the holdall. "Victory, I pray. Shake Scuttle awake."

Jason raised a hesitant hand. "Mr Poppal, there's something I forgot to tell you. Aunt Hester said that if *I* beat the pirates back to the house, she'd turn *The Slippery Skeggle* to splinters. Scuttle doesn't know. I'll be double-crossing him."

Mr Poppal laid a hand on Jason's arm. "Aunt Hester is an evil creature. Evil never plays fair. Even if the pirates were to bring her the stone, we could not trust her to deliver the boat. Wake your pirate. We must get started."

Jason tugged Scuttle's whiskers to startle him awake. At the sight of the stone the pirate turned instantly into a dog and clamped the gem in his slavering jaws. "Come, boy, the task be upon us," he slobbered.

"What's my job?" Mr Webberly asked, his teeth chattering like typewriter keys.

"You will be our lookout," Mr Poppal said. He opened the sun roof and lifted Swivel down. "Sound your horn if the pirates come. Are you ready, Jason?"

Jason nodded.

"Then go, my friend. And may all that is good in this world be with you."

Jason gulped and clicked his door open. "I love you, Dad," he whispered.

"Yes, well, chin up," Mr Webberly whispered back.

And then Jason was gone, with Scuttle at his side.

Thirty seconds later they were at the house.

Jason rang the bell. Mrs Webberly came to the door. She was still in her apron, and now she had a pair of rubber gloves on too.

"Ah, Jason. Good. About time you got back. Come along, your tea's nearly ready. We're having boiled cockle soup and seaweed stew. You can help me butter some coral wedges." She quickly stepped sideways in front of Scuttle. "No filthy dogs in the house, *thank you*."

The seadog growled and put the stone on the step. "I be bringing the gobbet," he grizzled.

"Mum, you've got to let him in," said Jason. From the corner of his eye he saw Mr Poppal sneaking through the bushes, heading for the rear of the house. "Scuttle's on his piratey task."

Mrs Webberly was not impressed. "I don't care if he's delivering piratey pizza. I've just mopped this hall and I'm not having mucky paws all over it."

"STAND ASIDE!" a hard voice rasped.

With a swirl of salty wind the door crashed back against its hinges. Aunt Hester was standing halfway down the hall. As the saltstone sparkled its light into the house, she bathed in the rays, absorbing their power. Almost immediately, the repellent fishy monster that Jason had witnessed earlier in the cellar began to take shape again. Aunt Hester's wrinkled flesh began to splinter and crack. Scales appeared as the skin flaked off. Fins grew in place of her ears. Her bulging yellow eyes, now as big as marbles, started swimming in their sockets like egg yolks slithering around in teacups. Seaweed sprouted in place of her hair. Her hands, though webbed, had long suckered fingers; they stretched and flexed like octopus tentacles. The Skegglewitch was growing right out of her. Jason had never been so scared in his life.

"Mum, get away!" he shouted. This wasn't any part of Mr Poppal's script, but sheer terror was ruling Jason now.

Mrs Webberly looked at him perplexed. "Jason, I have a sackful of albatross feathers to comb, not to mention a cauldron of fish bones to steam. I'm far too busy to be swanning off."

"But Mum, look at Aunt Hester!"

Mrs Webberly turned around. "Tsk, tsk," she tutted, pottering down the hall. "You really must do something about *these*, my dear." She pulled a snail out of Hester's nose.

That was it for Jason, he could take no more. "Here,

207

take the flipping stone!" he cried, and hurled it down the hall.

Typically, his aim was poor. Instead of walloping into the Skegglewitch, he managed to smash a souvenir plate from Ingoldmells.

Mrs Webberly clucked like a hen and immediately bent to retrieve the stone.

"Leave it and return to your duties," growled Hester, making a circular motion of her hand.

Mrs Webberly twitched. A dizzy look came into her eyes. "But it's untidy. I must clear the mess. That is my duty."

"YOU MUST NEVER TOUCH THE STONE!"

"Oh well, if you put it like that," huffed Mrs Webberly, and she tidied the broken plate instead.

Aunt Hester put out a slithering tentacle. The saltstone rose from the ground to meet it. "Ah," she gurgled, drawing it to her. "At last, the power is mine."

"OK, you've got what you want," quaked Jason. "Now turn Mum and Kimberley back."

"I be taking *The Slippery Skeggle*," barked Scuttle. "And…and…" He scurried round and round as if chasing his tail. Then in a furious voice he cried, "Treachery! I be stuck! I be a mangy cur! I not be able to toggle to a pirate. I be crossed most foul!"

Just like Mr Poppal warned us, thought Jason. "Where's Kim?" he shouted, bravely stepping forward. "What have you done with my sister?"

"*Beached*," the witch spat. "Prying little gnat. As for the boat…" She waggled a finger at a circular mirror built into the dresser halfway down the hall. The mirror cleared like a tiny pool. It showed a long black breakwater reaching out into a crashing sea. On the end of the breakwater, buffeted by wind and growling tide, was the ship's bottle.

"When the tide rises fully," Aunt Hester sneered. "The sea will take the ship *and* your sister. They will both be lost forever!"

"That's not fair!" Jason cried hotly. "We brought you the stone. That was the deal."

"FOOLS!" cried the Skegglewitch, rattling her scales. To Jason's horror, her bottom half began to shimmer. Slime began to ooze to the floor around her feet. Except she didn't have feet any more: she had a tail instead. She danced on it briefly, just as an evil mermaid might.

Yet the effect only lasted a moment. With another brief shimmer the tail disappeared and Aunt Hester found she had legs once more. She shook with fishy rage.

"The stone is tarnished. It is weaker than it should be.

You have been meddling, boy!" She fired out a tentacle and wrapped it tight around Jason's neck. "I will stew you in a whelk's shell and eat you for my supper. WHAT TRICKERY HAVE YOU DONE?"

"N-nothing," squawked Jason, barely able to breathe.

Somewhere in the distance a horn blared. *The pirates.* The pirates were coming.

Aunt Hester whipped the tentacle back. She raised the stone to her mouth. "I must test it," she gabbled, her eyes swimming wildly. "Seek out the power. There are grains on the surface. More must be buried inside." She clamped her teeth down hard on the rock. There was a horrible splintering sound. Jason thought at first the rock had cracked. But when he looked up, a shower of gubbins was falling from Aunt Hester's mouth. Her teeth had crumbled to dust.

"Treafery!" she screamed and hurled the saltstone at the wall. It shattered into a thousand fragments, bringing Mrs Webberly out of the kitchen.

"Tch, dustpan and brush," she tutted. "Left them on the landing I think." She pottered upstairs to find them.

The Skegglewitch convulsed with rage. She struck an old fishing creel, sending it bowling down the hall. "Poifoned," she croaked, like a sore-throated crow. "The ftone haff been tainted wiff finegar!"

Vinegar? thought Jason. *How had vinegar got on to the stone?* The reason soon became clear.

"Aunt Hester," said a clear, bold voice.

The Skegglewitch whirled around. "What iv thiff?" she snarled.

"Lemon juice," Mr Poppal said calmly – and squirted her with a lemon-shaped squeezer.

To Jason's astonishment, the wussely old fish began to steam. She screamed in agony, flapping every fin and tentacle she possessed. Suddenly, Jason understood why Aunt Hester never let anyone have vinegar or lemon juice on their fish – it was poisonous to her. That must have been the 'vital information' Dad had passed on to Mr Poppal.

Mr Poppal had another surprise for the witch, one that had come direct from his chip shop. "And this is batter!" he cried. He quickly unscrewed the plastic bottle of cream-coloured liquid and splashed it over Hester's fishy half. "My name is Sebastian Ffoulkes!" he roared. "And I have come to avenge my men!" Reaching down, he now pulled the leather pouch from his bag. He tugged the drawstrings. The pouch fell open. The hall filled up with a brilliant light. Its source was a fabulous silver-blue stone.

"This is the true saltstone!" he shouted. "The other is a

fake, as you have discovered. A few grains lacquered on vinegared shingle. Just to slake your vanity, Aunt Hester!"

The Skegglewitch let out a fearsome hiss.

Mr Poppal – Sebastian Ffoulkes – advanced, lost in a kaleidoscope of blue-white rays. "I have long been a scholar of the stone," he said, "and I have uncovered many of its secrets. It is said that when sunlight strikes the crystals, they reflect unimaginable heat. Look to the window, Skegglewitch. It is time to die – or rather, to fry."

Mr Poppal thrust the stone upwards. Jason saw at once what he was trying to do. He was hoping to catch the afternoon light from the tall stairs windows and reflect the heat back on to Aunt Hester.

But he had reckoned without the Skegglewitch's maid.

"Goodness," Mrs Webberly said. "Hasn't it got bright in here?"

To Jason's horror, she drew the curtains.

The Skegglewitch threw back her head and cackled. The whole of Shingle Towers shook.

Mr Poppal took a step backwards. Sweat glistened freely on his steep, bald brow. Now he was helpless, even with the stone. Helpless against a Skegglewitch.

With a roar Aunt Hester twisted her body till a mini-tornado was rattling the hall. The barometer casing fell to the floor. Paintings and ornaments flew off their hooks. The Welcome mat flipped like a dead autumn leaf. Everything whisked towards the ceiling.

Mr Poppal clawed against the wind. "Jason, run! We are lost!" he cried. With one last effort he hurled the saltstone into the air. The Skegglewitch reached up to catch her prize, only to see it taken from her grasp – by the ever-courageous Swivel. Swooping down from the swinging lightshade, he grasped the saltstone in his claws and flew away with it into the kitchen.

"You ufeleff bag of fefferf!" screamed Hester. "I will turn you into a fparrow for that!"

By now Mrs Webberly had returned to the kitchen. She issued a sharp rebuke to the bird. "Oh, shoo! Go away! No parrots in here. Oh now, what's *this* you've dropped?"

"No!" screamed the witch. "You muft not touch it!"

"YES, MUM! YOU SHOULD!" Jason screamed louder. He belted in to the kitchen. Suddenly, a light had gone on in his brain. What was it Aunt Hester had said when they were down in the cellar? *Your little sprat of a sister would pose a far greater threat than—* Than me, a *boy*, Jason thought. But Kim was a girl. And so was Mum. A very *big* girl. A girl with the Skegglewitch's *blood* in her veins. Mum had always said that the women

213

in her family were special. Now was the time to prove it.

"Mum, take your gloves off!" Jason shouted. "Feel the stone against your skin."

Aunt Hester made a gargling noise. "No," she hissed. "She muft not haff it." She lifted her hands to knock out a spell when the door burst open and the Salt Pirates of Skegness poured in.

"Stand by to skirmish!" Captain Blackhead roared.

Sadly, it wasn't much of a skirmish.

The Skegglewitch turned on them and croaked:

By eye uff frog and turnip root,
turn thefe piraffs into newtf!

With a flash, every pirate turned into a newt.

Aunt Hester whipped around, aware of someone wheezing behind her. A badly-winded Mr Poppal was trying to reach his lemon squeezer.

"For you, a fpeffle treat," gummed Hester. Her eyes rolled wickedly in their sockets. "I will turn you into a halibut and watch you fuffocate where you flap."

"Oh no you won't," said a voice.

Mrs Webberly walked calmly out of the kitchen. She had Swivel on her shoulder and the saltstone in her gloveless hands. Jason was touching it too. "Thank you," said his mum. "You can let go now. That's quite enough thought transfer. I think I've got the picture."

Aunt Hester smacked her gums together. "Fee to your dutif! Now!" she rasped.

"My duty is here," Mrs Webberly said. She held the saltstone out. Its light was not as bright now, Jason noticed. But a pulsing halo had formed around his mum. She was absorbing the saltstone's power. When she spoke there was a ghostly echo to her voice, as if the whole world was hers to command. "This is an interesting object, isn't it?" She opened her hands and the saltstone turned in the space between them. "It makes you feel very special, doesn't it? You know, I always did think I had an incy-wincy bit of *magic* inside me. And you never let on, *did you?*"

"You cannot fight me!" The Skegglewitch hissed. She put back her head and shot out a stream of wussely goo.

Mrs Webberly raised a hand. As the goo struck her palm she turned it to a cloud of harmless confetti.

"Yes!" went Jason, clenching a fist. "Go get her, Mum. You can do it."

For the first time, the Skegglewitch began to quake. "My dear, we can talk about thiff," she said.

"You're not nice," Mrs Webberly said. "You turned my daughter into a pebble."

"I am the fkegglewitch!" the Skegglewitch roared.

"You will giff me the ftone!"

Mrs Webberly calmly pushed up her sleeves. "No, I think *you* will give *me* the stone." And she twizzled the rock in her fingers again, making it send out a searing light.

The beam struck Aunt Hester, turning her blue. She let out a despairing squeal. Jason looked on in fear and amazement as a crater slowly formed in the centre of her chest and that part of her body began to disintegrate. Before long an actual hole had appeared. It grew steadily in size until Jason could see straight through it to Mr Poppal on the other side.

"What's happening?" he gasped.

Mr Poppal staggered to his feet. "The stone is reclaiming what it lost," he said, as a second hole appeared in Aunt Hester's thigh. A stream of salt came snaking out and leapt across the gap to join the stone. Every grain was absorbed into the body of the rock. It pulsed faintly with each new delivery. "All the grains Aunt Hester has eaten have been stored away in her body. Look!"

Aunt Hester was disappearing fast. Holes were popping up all over her now. And still the salt continued to flow, like sand through a large egg-timer, until there was nothing left to come out and she looked like a giant cheese grater on legs.

With an effort, she managed to move her mouth. "Piraffs," she moaned. "I hate piraffs. I will return…" she added spookily.

Then she collapsed into dust. And was gone.

Two seconds later, Mr Webberly arrived. "I'm armed and I'm coming in!" he cried. He crashed in brandishing a garden hose. "Where's the Hesterthing?" he panted, poking the hose about the hall.

Mrs Webberly pointed to the heap on the floor. "Don't stand in her, Brian, or swill her away."

"Or squash any newts," Mr Poppal advised.

Mr Webberly stepped back as a newt with a hooked claw skittered over his foot.

"Where's Scuttle?" muttered Jason. "What happened to him?" Only now did he remember that he'd seen the seadog sneaking out of the house just before Mr Poppal had launched his attack.

"I saw him heading for the beach," said Mr Webberly.

Jason gasped. "He must have gone for the boat!"

"I'd say you were right," Mrs Webberly said, frowning, "judging by the mess he's making on my floor." She nodded at the doorway.

The bedraggled figure of the seadog Scuttle came flip-flopping down the hall. Water was dripping off his sea-drenched fur. Small marine creatures were clinging to his ears. A piece of kelp was wrapped around his tail. He lowered his head and opened his jaws.

A pebble clattered on to the tiles.

"Kim," breathed Jason.

The exhausted seadog snorted a bubble of water from his nose. "I be caught 'twixt the boat and the pipkin," he panted.

Jason's bottom lip started to tremor. "You rescued Kim. You saved her life." A salty tear ran down his cheek.

"The boat?" said Mr Poppal. "What became of that?"

Mrs Webberly turned the stone in her hands. A twinkle of saltlight hit the mirror. A picture of the raging sea appeared. Waves were thumping the breakwater now, sending plumes of sea spray high into the air. Suddenly, a huge wave clawed at the wood and the mirror was awash with water for a second. Then the tide ebbed back and the stout black barrier appeared once more. The ship's bottle was nowhere to be seen.

Scuttle threw back his head and howled.

In the distance the grey sea crashed and every gull along the coast seemed to take up the cry.

Years later, local legend would describe how the utterance of grief was so long and so loud it could be heard all the way from the Skegglewitch's lair to the clock tower at the centre of Skegness...

One day later...

Chapter Twenty Six

"Mummy, can we go to the seaside today and see if we can see the piratey ship?"

"No," said Mrs Webberly, settling at the table.

Kimberley stabbed her fork into a bean. "Can we go on our *holly days* to the piratey ship?"

"No," said Mrs Webberly. "Eat your tea, please."

"But Mummy, I *like* the piratey ship!"

Mrs Webberly gritted her teeth. "I wish I'd left you as a pebble," she muttered.

Kimberley pouted her lip.

Mr Webberly ran a hand over Kimberley's head. "Sweetheart, that was yesterday. The pirates have all gone away now, pipkin. *The Slippery Skeggle* is their ship, not ours. Aren't you glad that Mummy made you big again? Aren't you pleased to be home?"

Kimberley frowned and swung a leg. "I want to go to Grobblymock Island!"

"Grubblemuck," said Jason, chewing his pizza.

"Don't encourage her," Mrs Webberly said quietly.

"I want to ride on *The Slobbery Squoggle*!"

Mrs Webberly said, "You're slobbery enough." She took a tissue from her sleeve and wiped a streak of cheese off Kimberley's chin. "No one is going anywhere on anything. We've had quite enough excitement for one weekend. We're going to sit here and eat our tea in peace. Aren't we, children?"

Jason glanced at his dad. Mr Webberly was looking a bit put out, clearly wondering if he was included in the child count or not. "I still say it was a risk," he muttered. "Getting that pirate ship out of the bottle."

"It was brilliant," Jason put in. The restoration of *The Slippery Skeggle* was almost the highlight of the weekend for him. As soon as they'd discovered the bottle was lost, Mrs Webberly had ordered Scuttle to stop whining and follow her down to the beach. Standing at the water's edge, with the tide just lapping around her shoes, she had performed a simple spell that had made the floating bottle pop its cork. The boat had appeared a few moments later, breaking the waves like a whale rising. Jason and Scuttle had almost smashed the sound barrier with their whoops (and woofs) of joy. Mr Poppal, holding the newts in a bowl, had nodded grimly and shed a quiet tear. Privately, he admitted to Jason that seeing the pirates' ship again had sent a wave of discomfort through him. But the time for reprisals had passed, he'd said; releasing the ship was right and proper.

As for the newts, they had careened around the bowl so much that Mr Poppal had been forced to spill them on the beach for fear of serious injury. Mrs Webberly had promptly restored them to pirates.

"What worries me," Mr Webberly said, "is what's going to happen if Blackhead and his crew don't obey orders and return the stone to this Grubblemuck place? What if they decide to do the dirty on us and run off and rove the high seas again, plundering and despoiling and making mayhem? They are pirates, after all."

"They're not *salt* pirates, though," Jason pointed out. (Mrs Webberly had lifted that curse in the change.) "They don't need the stone any more, Dad."

"They wouldn't dare disobey," Mrs Webberly said tautly. "Besides, Captain Ffoulkes will keep them in check."

Mr Webberly dug a little wax from his ear. "I still can't believe he wanted to go with them."

"It was his destiny," said Jason. "That's what he told

me. He said returning the saltstone to its proper place would be a debt of respect to the sailors who'd been lost on his ship."

"Well that's fair enough," Mr Webberly said. "But who in their right mind wants to take command of a filthy bunch of pirates and a moth-eaten parrot?"

Jason mopped up some sauce with a chip. "The pirates *wanted* him to lead them, Dad. Mr Poppal – I mean, Captain Ffoulkes, is clever and brave; he would have beaten the Skegglewitch on his own if Mum hadn't swished the curt…"

Jason's words tapered off as his mother gave him a bit of a look.

"…and he really loves Swivel. He says they're going to grow old together."

"Quite right," Mrs Webberly said. "That parrot was the real hero of the hour. He deserves a little tender loving care."

"I *like* parrots," Kimberley declared (she'd been stuck on a piece of pizza for a while and had therefore remained uncommonly silent). "Can we have a parrot for Christmas, Mummy?"

"No," said Mrs Webberly, buttering bread.

"Aunt Fester had a parrot."

"Aunt Fes— Aunt Hester has gone away."

"That's another thing," Mr Webberly said, crossing his arms and frowning hard. "Turning the old bat into a figurehead was not a good idea in my opinion."

Mrs Webberly poured herself a strong cup of tea. "She wanted to be a mermaid, didn't she? She can see the sea as much as she likes from now on."

Jason snickered into his fist.

Mr Webberly tightened his shoulders and shuddered. "She looked spooky, stuck on the front of that boat. I still say we should have hoovered her up."

"I decide what gets hoovered and what doesn't," said Mrs Webberly. "Now, can we please get on with our tea and have no more talk about pirates or witches." She cut a slice of bread into fingers and pushed them in front of Kimberley's plate. Kim made a rather rude noise with her lips.

Mrs Webberly sat back, wagging a finger. "Do that again, young lady, and those lips will gum right up."

Prruurrrpppp! went Kimberley.

Mrs Webberly twiddled her fingers.

Kimberley's lips gummed up.

"Flipping heck," said Jason, blinking with shock. He leaned forward to look at his sister. "Mum, did you—?"

Mrs Webberly twiddled her fingers again.

Kimberley's mouth popped open.

"Now," said her mum. "Do as you're told."

Kimberley pouted and speared a chip.

Jason and his dad exchanged a worried glance.

"Erm, dearest," Mr Webberly asked cautiously, "are you quite sure you've fully shaken off the effects of the saltstone?"

Mrs Webberly lifted her head. "Quite sure," she said. "Don't forget you're mowing the lawn this afternoon."

Mr Webberly flagged a hand. "I'll do it tomorrow. There's football on the telly."

Mrs Webberly stared at him hard.

"On second thoughts," Mr Webberly said, rising dizzily from his seat. "There's no point putting off till tomorrow what you can best do today, is there? Make hay while the sun shines, that's the spirit. Chop, chop. Get a move on, Brian. Oh, I do love the smell of newly-mown grass…" And with that he pottered off into the garden.

Jason immediately rounded on his mother. "Mum? *You* did that, didn't you? You've become a Skegglewitch, haven't you?"

Mrs Webberly swallowed a mouthful of pizza. "That's for me to know and you to find out, Jason. No more smashing things, all right?"

Jason gulped and bit his lip. "Mum?" he asked quietly, a hint of suspicion entering his voice. "You know yesterday when we were on the beach and you were turning everything back to normal and you said the only thing you couldn't do was change Scuttle back to a pirate 'cos Aunt Hester's curse was too strong to break and Scuttle would *have* to stay a dog for the rest of his days – you were FIBBING, weren't you?"

Outside, the mower thrummed into life.

A voice immediately bellowed: "BLISTERING BARNACLES! I be snuzzly as a snail in a seashell then!"

"Oh no, he's awake," Jason muttered.

Two seconds later, the old salty seadog was in the kitchen and sitting up on the vacant chair.

"Paws off the table," Mrs Webberly rapped. "You might be in my good books, dog, but you're not excused manners."

"Fuzzlewuck," the seadog grizzled. "What vittles be these?" He looked down at Mr Webberly's plate.

"Pizza," said Jason. "But it's not very salty."

The seadog twizzled a wiry ear. "Lately, I be right off salt," he said. He licked his lips and beamed at the pizza. "STAND BY TO BE BOARDED!" he barked.

And wolfed it down in one.

About the author

A-haar! Gather round, me hearties, for I be telling 'ee the tale of Chris d'Lacey, who be born on the middling day of December, 1954. This be making him right ancient and cobbly. He be creaky as the timbers on *The Slippery Skeggle*.

It be said he be slinging his hammock in Leicester, a land-lubbing hamlet from whence as a boy he did travel to Skegness many times in a chariot. He be right partial to seaside chips, but he be toggling his nose at cabbages and sprouts.

He be known to keep a pestersome pigeon or two. There be a strange hornswoggling legend afoot that he did once spin a yarn about such birds and did all but smuggle off with the medal of Carnegie, a sparklesome treasure amply revered by book worms and quaggle ducks.

He be married to a fearsome Skegglewitch (who be making him a frog the instant she be reading this) though he not be podding pipkins of his own. 'Tis reckoned he aspires to settle his bones on Grubblemuck Island, there to be singing many a shanty.

If you liked *The Salt Pirates* look out for another romp of
a read from Chris d'Lacey,

The
Fire
Within...

1 84121 533 3
£4.99

David soon discovers the dragons
when he moves in with Liz and Lucy.
The pottery models fill up every
spare space in the house!

Only when David is given his own
special dragon does he begin
to unlock their mysterious
secrets, and to discover
the fire within.

"Well, here we are," Mrs Pennykettle said, pausing by the door of the room she had for rent. She clasped her hands together and smiled. "Officially, it's our dining room, but we always eat in the kitchen these days."

The young man beside her nodded politely and patiently adjusted his shoulder bag. "Lovely. Erm, shall we take a look…?"

"It used to be our junk room, really," said a voice.

Mrs Pennykettle clucked like a hen.

The visitor turned. A young girl was lolling in the kitchen doorway. She was dressed in jeans and a sloppy top and had wet grass sticking to the heels of her trainers. "All our rammel's in the attic now."

"And where have *you* been?" Mrs Pennykettle said.

"In the garden," said the girl, "looking for Conker."

"Conkers?" the young man queried. "Aren't you a week or two early for them?"

"Not *ers*," said the girl, "*er*."

The visitor furrowed his brow.

Mrs Pennykettle sighed and did the introductions: "David, this is Lucy, my daughter. I'm afraid she comes as part of the package. Lucy, this is David. He's here to see the room."

Lucy chewed a wisp of her straw-coloured hair and slowly looked the visitor up and down.

Her mother tried again: "We've done the room out as best we can. There's a table in the corner, with a study lamp, of course, and a wardrobe we bought from a second-hand shop. The bed's not brilliant, but you should be all right if you try to avoid the loose spring in the middle."

"Mum?"

"*What?*"

"Why don't you stop twittering and *show* him?" With a huff, Lucy stomped down the hall to join them. "She's not always like this," she said to David. "It's because we've never had a lodger before." Before her mother could "twitter" in protest, Lucy reached out and pushed the door open. David smiled graciously and stepped inside. The fresh smell of lavender wafted through the room, mingled with the peaceful tinkle of wind chimes. Everything was perfect, exactly as described. Except…

"What's that?" David pointed to a bulge in the bed.

Elizabeth Pennykettle groaned with embarrassment. She swept across the room and dived beneath the folds of the red patterned duvet.

"That's Bonnington, our cat," Lucy said, grinning. "He likes getting under things – newspapers, duvets, all sorts of stuff. Mum says he's always getting under her feet."

David smiled and put down his bag. "Bonnington. That's a really good name for a cat."

Lucy nodded in agreement. "Mum named him after a mountain climber. I don't know why; he couldn't climb a beanbag. Well, he *could*, but we don't have one. He mistakes the sound of the beans for cat litter, then he poos on there instead of in his tray."

"Lovely," said David, glancing anxiously at the duvet.

With a rake of claws against fresh bed linen, Mrs Pennykettle emerged clutching a brown tabby cat. Her curls of red hair, now in total disarray, resembled a rather bedraggled mop. She grimaced in apology, plonked Bonnington on the windowsill and bundled him ungracefully into the garden.

David moved the conversation on. "Are there buses to the college from here?"

"Loads," said Lucy.

"Three an hour," her mother confirmed, hastily re-plumping her hair. "And there's room in the shed for a bike, if you have one. If you were stuck, you could always have a lift into town in my car – as long as you don't mind sharing with the dragons."

A delightful story which skilfully blends realism and magic into a very satisfying conclusion.
Carousel

A magical book.
The Bookseller

The Poltergoose

1 86039 836 7

£4.99

Something's after Jiggy McCue!
Something big and angry and invisible.
Something which hisses and flaps and stabs his bum
and generally tries to make his life a misery.
Where did it come from?

Jiggy calls in The Three Musketeers and
they set out to send the poltergoose
back where it belongs.

Shortlisted for the Blue Peter Book Award

Hilarious.
Times Educational Supplement

Wacky and streetwise.
The Bookseller

The Killer Underpants

1 84121 713 1
£4.99

The underpants from hell – that's what Jiggy calls them, and not just because they look so gross. No, these pants are evil. And they're in control. Of him. Of his life!

Can Jiggy get to the bottom of his problem before it's too late?

Join Jiggy McCue and his pals Pete and Angie in this pant-tastically funny adventure!

This is the funniest book I've ever read.
Teen Titles

Quirky, cheeky fun that children will love.
Publishing News
Starred Choice

The Toilet of Doom

1 84121 752 2

£4.99

Feel like your life has gone down the pan?
Well here's your chance to swap it
for a better one!

When those tempting words appear
on the computer screen, Jiggy McCue
just can't resist. He hits 'F for Flush' and...

Oh dear. He really shouldn't have done that.
Because the life he gets in place of his own
is a very embarrassing one – for a boy.

Another loo-ny adventure with
Jiggy and The Three Musketeers!